IT STILL IS WHT IT IS: This is a work of fiction and this statement is included to inform the reader that any celebrity name(s), business name(s), location(s), product(s), and organizations that are stated in the content of this book are real. However, they are used in a way that is purely fictional.

JAZZY KITTY PUBLICATIONS
ITS STILL WHT IT IS
JERZ TOSTON

It Still Is Wht It Is

By Jerz Toston

Cover Art Created by KREATIVEGRAFIKS.COM

Logo Designs by Justin Ackerman

Editor: Anelda L. Attaway

Co-editor: Jerz Toston

ACKNOWLEDGMENT

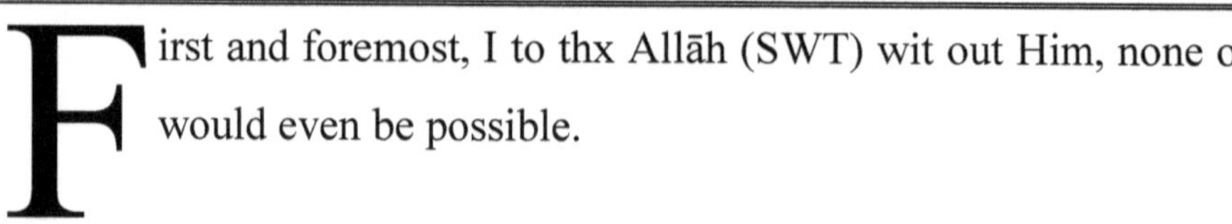

First and foremost, I to thx Allāh (SWT) wit out Him, none of this would even be possible.

DEDICATION

I dedicate this book to all my loyal fans because I appreciate their continued support and commitment to reading my books.

Ya Fav Author!

TABLE OF CONTENTS

INTRODUCTION

Urban Fiction at its best! The life journey of four couples: Jade and Ahmad, Bre and Maze, Turk and Fresh, and Killer and Lexis. Along with four friends, Fresh, Killer, Heem and Tiz, that had tha city in a chokehold because…. "It Still Is Wht It Is!" The continuation.

CHAPTER 1

It Still Is Wht It Is

"Aye yo Heem."

"What's up Tiz?"

"You need to check ya boy Gill."

"Why? What's up?"

"He's talkin' to tha bitches about biz-ness."

"Word?"

"Yeah, one of my young jawns told me her friend holla at him and all he talk about is us and how we got tha city on smash and how you be hittin' him with 10 to 20 birds."

"I don't even give that nigga more than 4 ½,"

"Just imagine if you did."

"I know, he's gon' fuck around and get us locked up or robbed wit his big ass mouth."

"I feel you on that, you know what they say, loose lips sink ships."

"Don't worry about it, I'll handle it."

"You know Ahmad and Jade are having a dinner Sunday?"

"He called me."

"I'm bout to holla at Fresh so make sure you handle that."

"No more said." We dapped each other and went on our way.

"Hello."

"Hey, Hey."

"What up Baby, I been waiting for you to call. I'm ready."

"That's what's up. Meet me at the back of Scooters."

"I'll be there in 30 minutes."

"Make it 20."

"20, it is then."

I shot to my stash house to pick up what I needed.

"Damn Nigga you tell me 20 minutes, but you take 40 I could have busted Tina's ass for another 10 minutes."

"Look, I ain't trying to know or hear that."

"You still be messing wit her peoples?"

"Yeah, I need to talk to you about that too."

"About what?"

"All that mafuckin' pillow talkin' you doing wit Tina."

"What are you talkin' bout?"

"Gill don't play dumb; you know exactly what I'm talkin' bout!"

"Nah, I don't."

"Well, let me jog ya memory."

"Hooold up Heem, we ain't gotta take it there. I was just trying to score some points wit Tina, that's all."

"Score some points? You dumb mafucka, you already knocked her off!"

"I know, but I wanted to make sure she wasn't going nowhere."

"By lying and putting our biz-ness out there?"

"It's only Tina, Heem."

"Do you see how she ran back to Janeen?"

"That's her girl."

"Nah because she dumb and young."

"Yo, she won't say nothing, I promise."

"I know she won't because I'm going to help her keep her mouth close."

"How are you gonna do that?"

"Like this." Pit, Pit, Pit, Pit. His head slammed back against tha headrest, then hit tha steering wheel. I got out, made sure nobody was looking, got in my car, then pulled off as if nothing ever happened. When I got back to the stash house, I unscrewed the silencer, cleaned it, as well as the pistol, then headed back out.

"Did you talk to Heem about that big-mouth young boy?"

"Yeah, I just left him and he said he would talk to him."

"We need to all sit-down and talk about a potential problem we might have brewing."

"What kind of problem?"

"Those Dominican cats. Call Heem and Killer, tell them to come thru."

We played Madden to kill time while we waited on Heem and Killer. When they arrived, we got straight to biz-ness.

"Those poppy mafuckas on tha hill are trying to step on our toes."

"How is that?"

"They got ounces for 500."

"That shit gotta be trash."

"From what I hear, it's a 6. Mafuckas jumping on it for that price."

"So what, we gonna lower our prices because of them?"

"Hell no, we gonna talk to them first. If that don't work, we'll take it to the next level."

For tha past 2 years, we been runnin' this operation. We haven't had any major problems, and tha one we did Ahmad advised us how to deal wit it. Ahmad and Maze were both deening and retired from the game, but I still went to them for advice.

"Heem, Heem!"

"Yo."

"Damn Nigga you ain't heard a word we said."

"You was in tha middle of tha highway with an 18-wheeler coming straight at you."

"You a'ight? Lexis told me about ya Nana."

"Yeah, but you know how that goes," I said, lying to cover what was really on my mind.

"You know we all family, so we're here for you."

"I know and I definitely appreciate it."

"So then tomorrow, I'll see if I can set up a meeting with them cats."

"OK."

"Now on to a few other things; them Niggaz on tha Ave and 30th have been repeatedly coming up short. We need to set an example so Niggaz don't think it's sweet."

"Evidently, they already do or else they wouldn't keep trying that shit."

"That's what happens when you try to fall back and just be on some money shit."

"Niggaz must of forgot we were goons before we started getting money."

"They think went soft."

"Well, it's time to let them and everybody else know we still the same Niggaz and It Still Is Wht It Is!"

CHAPTER 2

Who Hit tha Stash House

"Flacco we need to grab some more work this shit is going fast.

"Call Jose, tell him to get in touch wit Milan; this time we need 5 bricks."

"If shit keeps going like this, we should have the whole hill on lock in another 3 months tops."

"Those cats from down the hill sent word that they want to have a sit-down."

"About what?"

"I'm figuring it has something to do with us taking all this bread up here. You know they control close to 90% of the city."

"It ain't nothing to talk about but set it up somewhere neutral."

"I'll call Poppy and Jose so they can accompany us."

"Cool, I'll hit you back when everything is in place."

"If I don't answer, leave it on my answering machine and I'll get back wit you."

"Damn, I thought you would never hang up."

"I had to take care of some very important biz-ness."

"You got important biz-ness right here Flacco," she said, opening her legs exposin' her freshly shaved pussy.

Just the sight of it got me hard instantly.

"OOOOH Papi, I see somebody's excited."

Right when I was about to dive in face-first, there was a knock on the door. (Knock-knock)

"Who is it?"

"Javier."

"I'm busy come back."

"Boss its important, it can't wait."

"Hold that position, I'll be right back."

She took her fingers out of her pussy and into her mouth.

"I'll be right back."

As soon as he left, I called Heem.

"Yo, tell me something good."

"Nigga you gonna owe me big time for this shit."

"Just do what you got to do to get close to him."

"Don't worry by the time I'm done wit him he'll be begging to marry me."

"As long as you keep me informed, I don't care."

"I gotcha, you know that."

"Thanks Ma, you are the best."

"You can show me later when I stop by."

"Sounds good to me."

"Let me get off this phone before he walks back in."

"A'ight, see you tonight."

"Count on it."

"What tha fuck do you mean somebody hit our stash house?"

"Chico called me a few minutes ago wit tha news."

"What did they get?"

"15 grand and 2 ½ birds."

"They don't have any idea who did this or who was involved?"

"They had on masks."

"Evidently, they didn't give a fuck; they did it in tha middle of tha day! I need to find out who did this shit and fast," he said, punching a hole in tha wall.

When I walked back into tha room, Madi had already put her clothes back on.

"I'm sorry but an urgent matter came up."

"I figured that by all tha yelling you were doing."

"Can I call you later on tonight?"

"I won't be available tonight, I have to keep an eye on my grandma, she's real sick."

"No problem, I'll call you tomorrow. Maybe we can do lunch."

"You know tha number, just call."

"Take this wit you."

"I am not no prostitute or whore!"

"I know, I just want you to treat ya' self to something nice, now take it."

I grabbed tha wad of money, then left.

"Flacco I just got off tha phone wit Milan. Everything is in order for tomorrow."

"OK, did you talk to Jose?"

"No, why?"

"Javier said somebody hit tha stash house for 15 grand and 2 ½ birds."

"You mean to tell me nobody seen or knows nothing; that's bullshit. Somebody knows something."

"We'll find out soon enough.

"We talk to those cats down tha hill tomorrow at Jubilee around 2."

"OK, I'll hit you back; I need to handle a few things."

CHAPTER 3

Turk

"Thank you for tha breakfast Turk."

"No problem Mom. Would you like to go to tha nail salon wit me?"

"Sure, I could use a mani and pedi."

I pulled up to Larry's to drop my car off while I was in tha nail salon.

"Today must be my lucky day."

"And why is that Larry?"

"First Jade, then Bre, now ya fine ass."

"Boy, watch your mouth; you see my mom."

"I'm sorry."

"You just make sure you hook me up, especially my rims."

I had a 645CL charcoal gray on gray wit 22s.

"I'll be back in an hour."

"Hey Turk, Mrs. Taylor."

"Hey Jazz."

"How you doing Jazz?"

"Ok, Jade and Bre were here. But Larry already told you that, didn't he?"

"You know he did."

"Jazz hooked us up, so my mom tipped her."

Larry was just finishing up when we got back there.

"Is this tha same car," my Mom asked.

"Keep tha change, Larry."

"Thanks, you know Turk, if you...." I cut him off.

"No, thank you, Larry, my keys."

"Inside tha car."

As soon as we pulled off, "Turquis, can you blame him?"

I was a younger version of my mom, 5'7, dark skin, shoulder length hair, green eyes, yes, you heard me right, green eyes that were real, and an ass fatter than tha singer Beyoncé. A lot of people always mistake me for being Dominican.

"Turk, you can drop me off home, I'm tired."

"I thought you was gonna go to Philly wit me?"

"I was, but I'm tired now."

Once I dropped my mom off, I jumped straight on tha highway. As soon as I did, I wasted no time lighting up my weed. By tha time I got by tha Naamans Road exit, I remembered I had to meet tha cable man at 12 o'clock to fix my Internet service. I got off just to make a U-turn and get right back on. When I got to my house, tha cable man was just pulling up.

"Hi, are you, he looked at his clipboard, Ms. Turquis Taylor?"

"Yes I am."

"You're having a problem wit your Internet?"

"Yes."

I explained tha problem to him.

20 minutes later, it was back working.

"Thank you, I really needed that."

"Let me find out you're a YouTube, Facebook junky."

"Pleeease, I need my Internet to shop. Well, once again, thank you, I said, heading toward tha door.

I hopped in my car and headed to Philly to do some shoppin'.

CHAPTER 4

One or Two Options Deal or Die

"So, which one of you is in charge?"

"I'm in charge," Flacco said, standing up,

"Imma cut through all tha bullshit. This shit up here belongs to us."

"Hold on, my friend, we didn't put a gun to anybody and force them to deal wit us."

"True, you didn't, but you don't just come into somebody's hood and set up shop wit out permission."

"We don't owe you or anybody else shit!" Jose said standing up.

"Who tha fuck do you think you talkin' to?" Killer shot back.

Next thing I knew they both had guns drawn.

"Hey, hey, hey, no need for that," Heem said to Killer.

"Fuck this Gwala, Gwala beans and rice eating mafucka!"

"Jose Esta Bien! (It's a'ight)

"What tha fuck did you say?!" He asks now wit his other gun pointed at Flacco.

"Hold on Papi, no need for violence."

"You Goya Mafuckas got me twisted."

"You friend has a temper, I see."

"Heem let's cut to tha chase; you Niggaz got one or two options."

"We listen."

"You buy from us or you pack this show up and move on!"

"We have our own supplier. Maybe we can get you better numbers."

"9 outta 10 ya supplier is buying from us anyway. He's just stepping on it so much tha shits trash."

"I doubt that," Jose said, still ice-grilling Killer.

"You know what I know my man."

"What you know Papi?"

"You're no killer; I seen ya kind before you trying to hard this shit comes naturally."

"Then you know nothing my friend?"

But killer was actually right Jose was as soft as butter on a hot summer day.

"I'll give you 72 hours to decide. If I don't hear from you, I'll assume you chose not to deal with us and there for whatever happens happens. Come on, let's go."

'Tiz, Fresh, and Heem went out first while Killer backed out gun still in hand.

"It would behoove you to take us up on this offer. Then again, I'll enjoy killing ya bitch ass," he said, aiming his guns at Jose.

"I swear Imma kill that mafucka wit my bare hands."

"Calm down Jose calm down."

"Who do those faggots think they dealing wit?"

"No need to worry Milan is sending us some people down to help out wit this war we might have on our hands."

"If you ask me, I think we should grab 2 bricks off them just to avoid a war."

"Dominic that's some dumb shit; you always runnin' wit ya tail between ya legs."

"No I'm always thinking smart."

"Tell me how that's thinking smart huh?"

"We buy two bricks as a cover-up, but tha whole time we dumping our own shit; by tha time they catch on, we'll be too strong for them."

"Dominic, that is a good ideal. I'll call Milan to see what he thinks."

"Fuck 'em, if they want a war I say we give them what they want."

"We gotta be smart about this."

"Do you think they gonna deal wit us?"

"They really don't have a choice; either they do or they die, point blank."

"I hollered at them Niggaz from tha Ave and 30th they claim they been on point wit tha doe."

"I need to go over that way, so I'll pick that money up."

"You know they got that game in tha center later?"

"I kno I'll be there, I got a few pennies on it."

"You bet wit them cats from tha East Side, didn't you?"

"Sometimes you just talk cause you got a hole in ya face." (Ha! Ha! Ha!)

"Heem make sure you call Ahmad and put him down."

"I'm bout to hit him up now."

"Asalamu Alaikum"

"Wailakum Salam"

"How you?"

"I'm tayib." (good)

"Hum-du-Allāh." (All praise due to Allāh)

"We met wit them Dominican cats today."

"What's tha verdict?"

"They got 72 hours to get back wit us."

"Heem don't let them play you and what I mean by that is they're gonna front like they doing biz-ness."

"I thought about that and I'm ready for that."

"The question is, how long are you gonna let it go on before you do something? My man Milan hit me up wanting to do biz-ness I told him I'm not into that anymore, but I would pass his number along to you."

"Is he good money?"

"We would not be having this conversation now, would we?"

"Where is he from?"

"Philly."

"I'll holler at him; just give me tha number."

"Heem deal wit them wit a clear head."

"I will."

"Oh yeah, what's up wit you and Iciss?"

"Nothing."

"Don't let ya pride get in tha way of something good."

"I did what I had to do tha rest is up to her."

"I heard that Asalamu Alaikum."

"Wailakum Salam."

I can never get enough advice from Ahmad; he keeps me on my toes. I decided to call Milan to see what kind of numbers he was talkin' bout. I pulled out my burn out and punched in tha number from my iPhone.

"Hello," this guy said in a thick Dominican accent.

"Is this Milan?"

"Depends on who's askin'."

"This is Ahmad's brother."

"Oh, hello my friend."

"Hello. Can we talk?"

"As long as ya line is secure."

"In that case, we talk."

"I'm listening."

"I think we can help each other out."

"How's that?"

"I can be an asset to your biz-ness."

"I'm still listening."

"I would like to purchase 15 to 20 birds if it's tha same thing that I was buying from ya brother."

"Yup."

"When can I get them?"

"When do you want them?"

"A.S.A.P, you can meet me at tha Marriott by tha airport. Are tha number still tha same?"

"Depends on what the same is."

"27.5 apiece."

Since I knew Ahmad told me what he charged, I knew Milan was testing me.

"Nah, 25 a brick."

"Oh, in that case, bring me 20."

"No problem, give me one hour. I'll be in a black Marauder."

"OK, I'll be in a dark blue Yukon Denali."

As soon as I called Ahmad back, he let me know to have somebody follow me up wit tha work.

"Damn, give me a little credit."

"I know you smarter than that. I just wanted to make sure you were on point, that's all. Make sure you call me after tha deal goes down."

"Gotcha."

I called the Killer to ride wit me and my young boy Bagz to follow us wit tha work.

"You sure we can't trust this cat?"

"Yeah, he's Ahmad's peoples."

"That shit don't mean nothing, especially since he knows Ahmad isn't in tha game no more."

"I feel you, that's why I bought this," I said, pulling my .40 Cal out, "and you."

"Heem, I got a feeling them Dominican cats is on some funny shit."

"Me too, that's why I got a plan."

I hit Bagz and told him to get a room. Once he did, he took tha work up there, then brought me tha key.

"Here he comes now," I said, watching Milan pull in next to us.

He had two guys wit him. I motioned for him to get in. He hopped out, retrieve two duffel bags from his trunk.

"Hello Papi, nice to meet you. This is 500 grand; you can count it if you want to."

"My brother spoke for you, so I trust you."

"You have tha product?"

"Yup," I said, handing him tha room key.

"What is this some kind of joke?" he asked grabbing his bags.

"No that's tha room where tha work is and please turn tha key back in when you're finished."

"Papi you my friend are just like your brother, a smart man. I should be in touch in a few weeks."

"You know tha number, hit me up."

A hour later, Milan hit my phone.

"Yo, you definitely got a winner wit this."

"I know."

"I'll be getting wit you real soon."

Pop, Pop, Pop, Pop!

Boom, Boom, Boom!

Tat, Tat, Tat, Tat!

People were runnin' from every angle trying to avoid being hit.

"Who tha fuck started shooting?"

That's them Niggaz from River and Eastside beefing."

"I told you something was gon' to pop off every time they have this tournament at prices. It's always some dumb shit."

"Oh Shit!"

"What's up Fresh?"

"You bleeding."

Tiz looked at his arm and noticed he was bleeding.

"I think you were grazed; here take this and wipe your arm," I said, handing him my washcloth, "do you need to go to tha hospital?"

"Naw, I'm good, but I do need to find out who was shooting."

"It was Ty, Bones and Frog," some girl said, holding her arm.

"You OK Shawty?"

"Yeah, I was just run over when everybody scrambled trying not to get shot."

"You might wanna have that looked at."

"I'm bout to go to tha hospital now."

"Do you need a lift?"

"No, my car is around tha corner. Thanks anyway. You look like you need to go to tha hospital."

"I'm good, I was just grazed, nothing serious."

"What hand do you write wit?"

"Why?"

"Just answer tha question."

"My right."

"You not going to be able to drive so I'll drive you in ya car and you can have somebody meet you there to drive you home."

"How do I know you're not some kidnapper?"

"Do I look like one?"

"Who does nowadays?"

"My name is Tiz."

"I know ya name I heard my girls making a big fuss when yall walked up."

"Well, then you know I'm not a kidnapper." She just smiled, showing her cute dimples.

"Fire, Fire! Bitch, you had us worried to death."

"Yes you did, what happened to ya arm?"

"I was run over, but I'm OK."

"I guess you don't need us to drive you to tha hospital now?"

"Nah, but thanks anyway."

"It wasn't bout nothing; maybe I'll see you around."

"Maybe."

As we were about to leave, I heard one of her friends say bitch, I hope you got his digits.

I turned back around and asked, "Is it a'ight if I give you my number?"

"Sure, Neicy get my phone."

"Here, I'll put it in there for you."

"Take my number too."

"Nah, just take mines and if you call me then I'll have ya number. If you don't, I won't."

"I'll hit you up."

"Do me a favor, don't wait two or three weeks to call. Take me to tha crib so I can get cleaned up."

"Yo, Shawty name fits her to tha tee. She definitely fire."

She was 5'6", brown-skinned, brown eyes, hair to the back of her neck, hourglass figure wit a ass like Serena Williams. After I change, I need to shoot by River to see this Ty dude.

"Aye yo, what tha deal Fresh, Tiz?"

"We can't call it. Where tha boy Ty at?"

"Sitting on tha green box over there."

I walked over, "Ty let me get at you for a sec."

"Who you?"

"You was doing that shooting earlier and you hit me in tha arm," I said, showing him my arm.

"I wasn't the only one shooting."

"I know, that's why Imma holla at them other two Niggaz."

"So what you want wit me Playa?" he asked now hopping down off tha green box."

"A stack." (Ha! Ha! Ha!)

"You joking, right?"

"Do it look like I'm joking?"

"Nigga I ain't giving you no Fuckin' stack!" Before he could pull his pistol out my shit was in his face.

"Don't be no hero mafucka, Fresh take his pistol."

"Now like I was saying, a stack will compensate me unless you still don't want to give it up."

"You gotta do what you gotta do Cuz."

"Oh, you a tough mafucka, huh? Run his pockets Fresh."

"Damn, this little nigga, holding."

"See it wasn't about tha money its tha principle.

"Hey all yall come over here," I said to all tha little kids, "Fresh pass that shit out to 'em."

"You little mafuckas gone give me my money back."

"No, they not."

"Nigga shut up, you ain't no killer; if you was, I wouldn't have gotton hit."

"Imma see you niggaz again, only this time you won't be grazed!"

"Are you threatening me?"

"Take it as you want it."

"In that case." Boom!

Tha bullet from my .45 tour through his head, sending brain matter all over his boys.

"Anybody else got something to say? I didn't think so. If any of you Niggaz want to get at a real dollar, get at me."

"What's ya number?"

"My peeps over there got tha number. Don't take it if you ain't serious."

"Come on Nigga before the jakes come."

"Man they ain't going to be here no time soon. Like I said, if you not serious, don't waste my time."

CHAPTER 5

Tha Best Coke in the Tri-state

"It's been four days and you still haven't heard anything from them Dominican cats yet?"

"As a matter of fact, he called me this morning, but I was taking care of some other biz-ness at the time."

"Call 'em up."

"Hold up for a sec. these mafuckas must think this shit is a game, I see."

"Who that?"

"Ya boys from tha Ave, this is tha third time their paper is short; I'll be back."

"I'm going wit you; hold on let me grab my heat."

When we pulled up, they were all standing on tha corner by tha barbershop."

"Yo Beefy you seen Rell?"

"Heem, you know I don't fuck wit that nigga! He had to make a run; he should be right back."

"Imma wait for him if he on his way."

"Aye Heem you Fuckin' wit tha wrong mafucka."

"I know."

"Walk wit me to Kennedy Fried."

"Killer you always got your mad face on."

"That's cause Niggaz always trying to be on some bullshit. Let me get a three-piece breast and two wings."

"Heem word is yall got tha tri-state in a chokehold."

"I don't know bout all that, but we chewing."

"I'm trying to get at a dollar but my plug ain't consistent."

"Why you ain't holla at me then?"

"Ya boy Rell act like he didn't want to give it up. I know I just came home, but I'm not looking for no hands out. I got my own doe."

"How much you trying to grab?"

"I got enough for 9."

"Imma hit you wit tha whole brick."

"I told you I'm not looking for a handout."

"Somebody's going to have to run this shit, Rell is history."

"There that Nigga is."

"Yo Rell, get ya bitch ass over here!"

"Who tha fuck you talkin' to?"

"You! Now get tha fuck over here!"

"I don't know what his beef is, but you better holla at him Heem."

"We came to holla at you bout tha money you owe."

"What money?"

"Tha 15 grand!"

"I don't owe you no 15 grand."

"Tha last 3 times you been short 5 grand, so you do tha math."

"That's bullshit!" (Smack)

"Nigga who tha fuck you talkin' to."

"Mafucka you got me confused," he says swinging back on Killer but hitting his shoulder. His boy act like he wanted to jump in so I pulled out my .38.

"Give me a reason to put some hot shit in you."

"Handle ya biz-ness Killer." He pulled his 9 out and shot Rell in both his knee caps.

"AAAAAHH FUCK!"

"Stand ya bitch ass up."

"I-I-I-I can't."

"Make sure you hit me up Beefy."

"You know I am."

"Come on Killer we out."

"Imma see you; this is far from over," Rell said, "help me get in the car so I can go to tha hospital."

"I should of pushed his wig back."

"You did right, it was too many people out there. Somebody would have told for sure.

"You talk to Fresh or Tiz?"

"Not since earlier this morning."

"You know they got to shooting at the game and Tiz got grazed."

"Is he a'ight?"

"Yeah, he just wants to holla at tha Niggaz who was doing tha shooting."

"That can't be good."

"We'll know by the end of tha night."

It had just gotton dark out.

"Fresh pull up on Lombard; we can walk up tha block."

"Tiz what's good wit you?"

"I can't call it. Jam you seen Frog or Bones?"

"Them Niggaz be down on Bennett between 9th and 10th."

"A'ight, good looking."

"They owe you some money?"

"Nah, they were shooting at tha game today and I got grazed in my arm."

"Oh shit, that was them who was doing that shooting?"

"Yeah."

"A'ight, you be safe out here I'm bout to holla at them"

"Leave tha car we can walk tha couple of blocks."

"What you two Niggaz doin' over these parts?"

"Came to holla at you and Bones."

"What's up?"

"Yall was doing that shooting today?"

"That bitch ass nigga Ty started shooting first."

"Yeah, well somebody hit me in tha arm."

"Seriously?"

"Yeah."

"I don't know if it was us but will pay tha bill."

"Nah, I'm good I just wanted to let you know."

"Imma slump that bitch nigga!"

"Too late, I already handled that."

"Huh?"

"I went to holla at him just like I did yall, but he started runnin' his mouth like he was built like that."

"Damn, we owe you big-time for that."

"You don't owe me shit. Next time don't be so reckless, anybody could've gotton hit or even killed, for that matter."

"We were just defending ourselves; we don't do no dumb shit like that."

"I really didn't think yall did, but I still had to come holla at yall."

"True, I respect that. You could of came on some bullshit."

"I didn't know that lil' nigga, I know yall."

"Funny thing is, he was beefing over a bitch."

"Yeah right."

"Seriously, Frog was knocking his baby mom off. I didn't even know she was his peoples until tha nigga said something to her and she told me."

"They don't even mess around no more. He probably one of them DMX Niggaz 'I love my baby mama. I never let her go.'"

(Ha! Ha! Ha!)

"You crazy."

"But on another note, what tha money like over here?"

"Wit some good coke, we can lock this shit down."

"Who yall dealing wit now?"

"Them N.Y. cats up tha block."

"What they numbers like?"

"We only doing 13 ounces for 10.8."

"Well, I can do the same for 8,400 and tha work is tha best in tha tri-state area. I'll bring you something you can put out, if they like it which I know they will then we go from there. Deal?"

"I trust you, so bring me 16."

"Let me make a call and it will be here in tha next 20 minutes.

Frog yall got something?"

"40 minutes."

"I hope it's better than tha last stuff."

"Ma this shit they bout to get will definitely take 'em to new heights."

"I hope so, they my boys, but I can't keep buy'n that garbage."

20 minutes later, my young boy was pulling up.

"Bones get in tha car he'll take care of you."

"You want me to give him tha money?"

"Yeah."

"Do what you need to do we are going to stay out here."

"Are you sure?"

"Yeah, handle your biz."

"This that shit right here we got 21 ½ outta that."

"Ms. Patty come here."

"Yall ready?"

"Yeah."

"I need something for 60 dollars."

"Here, let me know what it's hittin' for."

"You know I am."

10 minutes later, Ms. Patty was back.

"Where did yall get this shit from?"

"You don't like it?"

"Hell no! I thought this was tha best shit in tha tri-state?"

"It is."

"Not according to Ms. Patty."

"Ms. Patty don't know good coke."

"Yes I do and this shit is tha best coke I ever had, trust me, I've heard a lot of good shit."

"Ms. Patty don't be playing with us like that."

"I was having a little fun wit yall, that's all."

"Now that yall know what it's hitting for, we out. Fresh, let me get ya number too."

"Yall gonna be ready when we done, right?"

"We never run out; just call."

"Now that's what I'm talkin' bout."

Ms. Patty spread tha word around the whole Eastside that we had that good stuff and before long, we had tha block jumping.

"Damn Frog, you should've been hollered at them Niggaz. We need to call 'em back. We only got 6 ounces left."

"Hold this shit down while I get the doe together and call Tiz."

"Yo, what's up, everything a'ight?"

"Yeah, you think you can swing back through?"

"You finished already?"

"Just about, I need a whole one."

"Give me 30 minutes Imma hit you wit 2 and just owe me 30."

I had no problem giving him an extra 5 since it was on consignment not to mention I was going to turn 36 into 48 easy.

"OK I'll be outside."

"When a call, meet me at Mr. Benny's"

"What he say?"

"I gotta meet him at Mr. Benny's when he call."

"Yo Bones, them New York cats ain't going to make no money."

"That's what we wanted."

"He also said he's going to front us a brick for 30."

"We should sell some weight a stack a ounce. On tha next flip, we gonna dime all this up and make a killing."

CHAPTER 6

Heem and Iciss

"Hey Brother, I got my results back from my bar exam."

"And?"

"And I passed; I am officially a lawyer."

"Take a ride wit me. I have to relieve Ms. Barb."

"She's OK?"

"She just asked me if she could get more hours."

"A'ight, where are we going?"

"Just come on."

"OK, OK I'm coming."

"Oh, I guess you would be needing these," I said grabbing the biz-ness cards out of tha glove box.

"When did you get these?"

"Tha same day you took tha bar I knew you would pass."

Iciss Jones attorney of law it had my cell and another number I didn't recognize along wit an address on it.

"Who's address is this?"

"Yours."

"Mines?" she asked wit a real puzzled look on her face.

"That's right," I said, pulling into tha parking spot reserved for Iciss.

When I read the sign in front of the building, all I could say was, "Oh My God!"

"Sis, like I said, I knew you would pass. Come on and check out ya office."

"Wow, this is really laid out."

"Jade and Mom Sady did all tha decorating." Tha phone started ringing.

"I've been giving out ya card so you might wanna answer that."

"Hello Iciss Jones."

"Hello Ms. Jones, I would like to put you on retainer."

"How do you know if I'm any good or not?"

"Simple, you come highly recommended, you're young, hungry, and trying to make a name for yourself."

"You'll have to come in so we can talk face-to-face."

"When will you be free?"

"How long will it take you to get here?" (Knock, Knock)

"Could you hold for a second, please?"

"Sure."

"Come in. Heem what are you doing here?"

"Are you gonna leave that caller on hold?"

"Oh shit. Hello, I'm sorry for tha wait."

"That's OK I'm here anyway."

She turned around to see Heem holding tha phone to his ear.

"Yall play too much."

"I'm not playing; I told you I wanted to put you on retainer if you passed."

"I thought you was joking."

I put a black bag on her desk and opened it.

"Does it look like I'm joking?"

"How much is this?"

"65 grand. Everybody else will be bringing their retainer fees too. My young boy got booked yesterday for trafficking, but they didn't find nothing on him. They found it in an alley and charged him."

"I'll get on it first thing in tha morning."

"How bout you let me take you to dinner to celebrate?"

"I don't know if my mom or sister have anything planned."

"They don't, go enjoy yaself tonight."

"Well, I guess we can have dinner. Ya treat, right?"

"How you gonna ask me to dinner then ask am I paying?"

"I just figured since you're about to come filthy rich it shouldn't be a problem, but don't worry I got it covered. I gotta run, but I'll pick you up around 8:30."

"A'ight, I'll see you then."

"You know he really likes you."

"I can't tell, if he did he would have asked you by now."

"He did."

"When and why didn't you tell me?"

"That night we went to Friendly's."

"That was almost a month ago."

"I know."

"Ahmad Imma hurt you."

"I didn't think it mattered since you told him you looked at him like a brother."

"OOOOOOH, he told you that?"

"Yup."

"I was just playing hard to get."

"Iciss let me ask you a question, do you like Heem?"

"As crazy as this may sound I love him and if you tell him Imma hurt you."

"That's funny, he said tha same thing."

"Really?"

"Iciss all I'm gonna say is follow ya heart and don't let something good get away."

"I hate when you're right."

"I'm always right."

"Don't remind me."

"You are my little sis, Imma always have ya back, no matter what."

"I know and vice versa."

"Come on let's get out of here."

"OK. I need to get back to tha store."

"No you need to get ready for your dinner date in a few hours."

"Ms. Barb's probably ready to leave."

"She's a'ight, she wanted more hours now she has them since you no longer work there."

"How you just gonna fire me?"

"I'm not firing you, but you're not going to have time to work in tha store once ya caseloads pick up."

"Until they do, I'll still come by and help out for free."

"Now that's a word I didn't know existed in ya vocabulary."

"Ha-Ha very funny."

"I'll talk to you later I'm about to go to tha masjid to offer prayer."

I was a little hungry but decided not to eat so I could enjoy my dinner wit Heem. I almost forgot to call Jade to let her know tha good news. When I called, nobody answered, then I remembered she was making Salat (prayer). I pulled up to my apartment just as my phone started ringing.

"Hey Mom."

"What you doing?"

"About to go in tha house and take a shower."

"Why don't you come over later for dinner."

"I would love to, but I already have a dinner date."

"You do, wit who?"

"Heem."

"Is that tha cute boy Ahmad calls his little brother?"

"You know who Heem is mom."

"I was just seeing if it was tha same Heem that I told you I could see yall together."

"Mom don't start it."

"I'm not, I'm just saying, I told you last year he liked you, now didn't I?"

"Yes you did, but just because he's taking me to dinner doesn't mean he's going to be your son-in-law."

"It's a start."

"Besides, he's only taking me out because I got my license to practice law."

"Yeah Yeah whatever; it's ya mom you talkin' to."

"Anyway, I'll stop by afterwards."

"If it's not too late."

"Goodbye Mom I love you."

"I love you too and congratulations."

"Thanks Mom."

I decide to smoke me a blunt and have me a little champagne to do my own celebrating. I looked at tha clock on tha wall, Shit I better get my ass in tha shower. Heem will be here in a hour. I didn't know where we were goin, so I just put on a peach sundress and open-toed shoes to match. I was feeling good from the champagne and weed, so I smoked another Dutch while I waited on Heem.

(Honk Honk)

I opened my front door and put my finger up, telling him to wait a minute while I put some eyedrops in my eyes.

"Hey, you look real nice."

"Thanks I didn't know we were going so I figured I could not go wrong wit this outfit."

"You definitely can't."

"So where are we going anyway?"

"It's up to you."

"Well since it's up to me, I say we go to Texas Roadhouse." All I did was smile cause Ahmad said she would pick Texas Roadhouse.

"What you smiling for?"

"I was just thinking all that time you was messing wit Dash I was secretly wishing it was me and if I ever had tha chance I wouldn't let it go to waste."

"I hear you."

"Nah for real, but once you told me you look at me like a brother I knew I didn't stand a chance so Imma fallback."

"I haven't been completely honest wit you."

"How so?"

She waited until I parked tha car so she could look me in my eyes and say, "Heem I really don't look at you as a brother. In fact, I've been liking you from tha moment I laid eyes on you. I just never knew if you felt tha same way and as crazy as this may sound, I love you."

I was speechless, so I just grabbed her face and kissed her so passionately to let her know I did feel tha same way. When we came up for air, we both smiled and got out.

"Damn, he is a hell of a kisser," I thought to myself.

"Close ya eyes."

"What?"

"Please."

"Only because you said please."

He guided me inside and helped me to our table.

"Now open ya eyes."

As soon as I did everybody yelled, "Congratulations!"

I couldn't believe it. My mom, Turk, Bre, Chas, Jade, Ms. Taylor, Alexis, Brazia, AJ, Maze, Fresh, Ahmad, Killer, Tiz, and Ms. Barb were all staring at me clapping.

"You knew about this tha whole time and didn't tell me."

"Now, if I told you then you wouldn't be surprised like you are now."

"Mom, you didn't even say nothing when we talked earlier."

"Aunty, congratulation," AJ said, not pronouncing it right.

"Thank you, Aunty's Baby. How did you know I would want to come to here?"

"It's ya favorite spot to eat."

"I could've wanted to eat somewhere different tonight."

"Then I would've had a taste for this." We all ordered.

"So who's paying for this tab?"

"Iciss," everybody said at tha same time.

"I guess we doing tha eat and run out thing cause I didn't bring no money out wit me."

"I got it," Maze said.

"Nah, we got it," Killer said.

"Iciss will be by tha office tomorrow to drop our retainer fee off."

"Fine by me."

"Well, since I need a job and you need a receptionist," Chas said.

"Ahmad you told her, didn't you?"

"I didn't say anything."

Jade looked at me, then said, "I might've mentioned it to Turk."

We ate, then sat around talking until Brazia and AJ fell asleep.

"We better get home it's way past their bedtime."

"Iciss you need a ride," Chas asked.

"Are you taking me home or do you have something to do?"

"You know damn well he taking you home," Turk said wit a smile.

"I wish they would stop playing all these games and just hook up," Chas said high fiving and Lexis.

"Mind yall biz-ness and stop worrying bout us."

"Man, this nigga been wanting to holla at you since he saw you."

"Yall make a cute couple," Ms. Barb added.

"Heem you better stop playing it before she gets away again."

"So yall gonna handle me like that? Just for that, yall not invited to my birthday party next month."

"How old are you gon' be?"

"22."

"You only a few months older than Iciss."

"Mom."

"Come on Iciss, I am ready to leave now."

"Me too, I'll talk to yall tomorrow."

"Don't forget we're going to drop that change off around 11 o'clock."

"I'll be there."

On tha ride home, neither of us said a word we let Maxwell do tha talking for us.

"So I guess I'll see you tomorrow?"

"Oh, you not coming in?"

"I didn't know you wanted me to."

"It's still early. We can watch the movie Brooklyn Finest you wanted to see unless you have somewhere you need to be or someone you need to be wit?"

"If that's ya way of asking if I'm seeing anyone; no, I'm not."

"If I wanted to know that I would've just asked. Are you coming in or not?"

"You're definitely gonna make one hell of a lawyer. You are ya sister's sister."

"What's that suppose to mean?"

"Stop being so defensive; all the time. All I was saying is yall have style."

"Make yaself comfortable while I put my night clothes on."

"Can I smoke in here?"

"Smoke what?"

"Weed."

"Go head, I thought you were talking about those nasty ass cigarettes."

"Hell no, I can't stand those things."

"Me either."

I washed up then put on my short Tweety Bird nightgown.

"Damn, you comfortable enough?"

"Yeah," I said, taking a pull of my Dutch.

"Let me have some."

"Some of what?" I asked, already knowing she was talking about tha weed.

"The weed, what you think I'm talkin' bout?" I smiled and held up my glass.

"I could use a glass of that too."

"I'll pour you a glass while you put tha movie on."

"Make sure you put a little ice in it please."

I could not help looking at Iciss in that Tweety Bird nightgown, especially when she bent over to put tha movie in and I noticed she didn't have any panties on. Since I know he's watching, let me give him something to look at. I bent over to get tha DVD exposing my ass. I couldn't help smiling to myself, knowing he got an eye full since I don't have on any panties.

"I hope that's enough ice for you?"

"Yeah, that's good. I hope you don't mind if I turn tha light off."

"I would if I was afraid of tha dark."

"I thought Ahmad said you slept wit a nightlight."

"Ha Ha very funny," I said, leaning back on tha sofa to get comfortable again.

Halfway into tha movie, Iciss slid next to me, laying her head on my chest.

"I could get used to this."

"Me too," she said, turning her head to look me in tha eyes, "Killer was right, I'm not letting you get away this time."

"I hope not," she said, then kissed me.

"Heem can you stay wit me tonight?"

"Only if that's what you want."

"I wouldn't have asked if it wasn't."

"I'll be happy to."

"Come on cause I'm going to bed. I have a long day ahead of me tomorrow."

I followed her to tha bedroom where I stripped down to my boxers and climbed in bed. I already made my mind up that I would just hold her tonight.

CHAPTER 7

First Court Appearance

Today was my first court appearance. I had a suppression hearing for Heems, young boy Bucky.

"All rise. Your Honorable, Judge Dixon, presiding you may be seated."

"As to case number 4032411 the state vs. John Gray, prosecution present ya case."

After they presented their so-called case, and I had a chance to cross-examine tha experts, I was sure that we would win.

"As for my decision, I have no choice but to grant this suppression and throw it out. Wit that said, Mr. Gray, you are free to go."

On my way out of the courtroom. I was stopped by this guy.

"Excuse me, can I have a minute of ya time?"

"Yes."

"How much do you charge?"

"It depends on tha case."

"I was pulled over and they found a gun in the trunk."

"Did tha car you were driving belong to you?"

"No, and tha gun didn't even have my prints on it."

"That's an open and shut case."

"I know but tha lawyer I got wants me to plea out."

"Listen, here's my card. Give my office a call so you can get an appointment."

"OK. Are you in court today?"

"Only for arraignment. Plead, not guilty and call as soon as you leave, give me ya name so I can get the paperwork while I'm here."

"Jason Gibson."

Walking out tha courthouse I felt good. I beat my first case and got a new client in tha process. Not to mention, I had the love of my life, Heem.

"Sunshine, ya brighten my life sunshine you make me feel a'ight."

"Hello."

"Hey Ma."

"Hey there."

"Where are you at?"

"Just leaving Court."

"Bucky called me; he said you ran circles around tha prosecutor."

"That's what I do. I also picked up a new client."

"That's my Baby. Did you eat this morning?"

"I had a cheese Danish."

"How about I pick you up for lunch in an hour?"

"That sounds good. That'll give me enough time to do what I need to do at tha office."

"See you in an hour."

"I can't wait."

"Them Dominican cats think we stupid."

"How so?"

"They been buying two bricks a week as a cover."

"A cover for what?" Fresh asked.

"They only copping two bricks so we won't go at their necks. They still doing biz-ness wit they people."

"How do?"

"I know because tha work I'm giving them is trash and they not complaining about it."

I put tha pistol to her sons head.

"Please don't hurt my son."

"That's up to you. now where's tha money at!"

"In tha attic."

"You dumb bitch Imma kill you if they don't!"

"Fuck you I'm not going to let my son die for yall!"

"Jackpot!" Rob yelled out.

One of tha guys on tha floor tried to make a move pit, pit, pit.

"I thought I said don't move."

"You better hope he don't die mafucka!" Pit.

"Looks like he just did."

Rob came down wit two duffle bags.

"There's one more up there."

"Yo, lets finish this and get up outta here."

"I'll take care of it hand me ya pistol."

Wit out saying another word, I put tha pistol to tha back of his head and pulled tha trigger, then did tha same to tha one who was doing all tha talking.

"What about her?"

"Pleeease don't kill me." I opened one of tha duffle bags took a stack of money and handed it to her.

"Take this and go. if you say anything about this we will kill you and ya son."

"I won't say shit you have my word."

"Come on lets get outta here."

"Remember Shawty if you tell this will happen to you and yours."

"Hey Madi."

"Hey Papi"

"I been trying to get in touch wit you for a few days.

"Me and Flacco went to tha Bahamas."

"I'm glad to hear you enjoyed ya self. did you find out anything I can use?"

"Not really, just that he deals wit somebody in Philly."

"Did he mention his name?"

"No, but he did say he was trying to take over tha whole, west side at all cost."

"A'ight I'll hit you in a few days . try to find out who his supplier is."

"I got you just relax; don't I always come through?"

"Madi Madi, he's calling me."

"Yes Papi."

"You stay here I need to go in town to check up on a few things."

"I need to go in town to get some clothes and check on my grandmom."

"You take my keys and come back when you're done."

"A'ight, I'll see you later.

Damn, this mafucka ain't answering his phone let me call Jose. after a few rings, his machine picked up.

"These Niggaz gonna make me snap when I get in town." I stopped by

Jose's house but his girl said she hadn't seen or talk to him in 2 days. I knew something was up because Jose always talked to his girl no matter what he was doing. I headed to swing by Dominic's house to see if he heard from Jose but got tha same results. I tried to stay positive but deep down I knew it was something wrong. when I got out tha car I could smell death in tha air. my worst fears became a reality when I walked thru tha front door. Jose, Dominic, and Joan were all laying dead on tha floor bodies decomposing."

"Couldn't hold it in, I threw up all over tha floor. I checked tha attic before calling tha police but everything was gone. after tha police came and questioned me I called Milan.

"What do you mean their all dead?"

"Just like I said dead and I don't have a clue who did it. I'm sending 15 of my men down."

"Do what you need to do to get tha answers you need."

"Right now tha police are everywhere."

"A'ight."

"Give me a few days and I'll send 'em down."

These mafuckas, want war we gonna see if they built for war! I headed to jubilee to get some drinks so I could clear my head.

"Flacco you back in town."

"Yeah, let me set some tequila matter fact bring the whole bottle wit a cup."

"What's wrong my friend you look like your heart is heavy?"

"Jose, Dominic and Joan were murdered."

"No I just see them two days ago."

"That's probably when it happened, I just found item about a hour ago."

"I'm sorry to hear that Flacco."

I sat there for tha next 4 hours getting wasted.

"Hello."

"Hey Papi, when you coming home!"

"I don't know."

"Are you drunk?"

"No, I'm not drunk, but I've been drinking a little."

"You sound drunk where are you?"

"Chubilee."

"Don't move, I'm on my way."

"Flacco sounded beyond drunk maybe I can get some information out of him now."

Flacco was drowning shots of tequila like they were cups of water.

"Is everything O.K.? I've never seen you drink like this before."

"That's because my friends weren't dead," he said in a drunken slur.

"Friends dead? What are you talking about?"

"Dominic, Jose, and Juan were murdered."

"Are you sure?"

"I found them myself; their bodies were decomposing."

"Let me help you so we can go home."

"I'm not done drinking."

"We can stop at tha LQ. and get another bottle."

On tha ride home, Flacco kept mumbling something about it's all his fault they were dead. I used this as an opportunity to get a few answers.

"Do you think it was those guys you said wanted you to buy their drugs?"

"I really don't know because all my money and drugs were stolen."

"Sounds more like a robbery to me because why would those guys take your money and drugs when they have their own?"

Even though I was inebriated, what she said, made a lot of sense.

"My People are sending me a small army in a few days; we'll get to tha bottom of this."

"I got people in Philly I can call to help Papi."

"No need, I have 15 people coming to help me."

"Do you need somebody to sell tha drugs, yes?"

"They'll do that too." I had to help him into tha house.

"Sit down, let me take ya shoes off. Are you hungry?"

"Yes."

"I'll warm you up something to eat."

I went into tha kitchen and called Heem.

"Yo this Heem leave it."

"Hey Papi hit me in tha morning. I got some information for you."

"Shit, I missed Madi's call. I listened to tha message she left. I put a mental note in my rolodex, so I wouldn't forget to call her in tha morning. I need to call Ahmad and check up on him.

"Asalamu Alaikum."

"Wailakum Salaam."

"What's good wit you Big Homie."

"Nothing. Just trying to put tha finishing touches on this restaurant."

"That's what's up; I didn't want nothing just figured I'd call since I hadn't talk to you in a few weeks."

"It's been that long?"

"Yeah."

"I guess Iciss keeps you occupied."

"Cut tha bull crap."

"According to Jade, when she's not at work, she's wit you."

"Ahmad, I got to keep it funky like a junkie sex; I should've been went at her."

"I'm glad you both happy cause at tha end of tha day, that's all that matters."

"True."

"How did you make out on that situation you had?"

"3 outta 4 ain't bad. You know they gonna send some help."

"I kinda figured they would. You just make sure you stay on point."

"No doubt, I'll hit you tomorrow. Asalamu Alaikum."

"Wailakum Salaam."

"Hello."

"Hey."

"I was just about to call you."

"Yeah right."

"I was after I hung up wit Ahmad."

"I was on a conference call wit Jade and my mom but I told them I had to call you."

"Now you trying to make me feel bad."

"No I'm not, I'm just being real."

"Are you home?"

"I'm just leaving tha office."

"At 8 o'clock?"

"I have to prepare for this trial I got coming up next week."

"I'll meet you at ya house. Did you eat?"

"No, not yet."

"I was about to grab something from Ahmad's do you want something?"

"Yes, you can get me tha steak & shrimp gyro wit some curly fries."

"A'ight, I'll be there in a little bit."

"Tha door will be unlocked."

Even though me and Heem have only been together for a few months it feels like an eternity. I asked Chas if she thought it was too soon to give Heem a key her response was 'I thought he already had one.'

"Asalamu Alaikum."

"Hey Sis."

"Hey."

"Was you busy?"

"No, just finished giving AJ a bath."

"I got a question for you."

"I'm listening."

"Do you think it's too soon to give Heem a key?"

"He don't have one already?"

"You sound like Chas. No, he doesn't have one."

"At first I thought you was gon' say it was too soon to give him some pu nanny."

"He hasn't got any of that yet either."

"Are you serious?"

"Yup, not that I haven't wanted to give him some; he just hasn't made a move."

"Ha! Ha! Ha!"

"It's not funny."

"I'm laughing because Ahmad was tha same way; I had to take it."

"Girl, you is crazy."

"It's tha truth, but once he got some he's been hooked ever since."

"So are you saying?"

"I'm not saying anything," she said, cutting me off, "what I will say is he respects you enough to wait til you're ready."

"He'll never know if I'm ready if he doesn't try."

"Remember what mom always told us? If you want something bad enough take it."

"Well, I'm about to take a shower so give him a key and call me tomorrow so we can do lunch."

"A'ight thanks, love ya Sis."

"Love you too."

I jumped in tha shower since Heem wasn't there yet. After tha long day I had tha shower felt really good. I had my mind made up. It was time to stop tha cat and mouse game we were playing.

"I locked tha door behind me after letting myself in. I was about to call Iciss, but I heard the shower so I knew it would be a waste of time, so I rolled me a Dutch. Once tha water stopped I called Iciss.

"Yes."

"I was just letting you know I was here, that's all."

"OK, I'll be right out. Is tha food still hot?"

"Warm."

"Put it in tha microwave for a few minutes for me, please."

"Gotcha."

Iciss came out and one of her many sexy Victoria's Secret nightgowns.

"I'm sorry, were you expecting somebody else?"

"Boy stop playing. You know I was I always wear these to bed."

"You're tha only female I know who always go to bed sexy."

"Is that a bad thing?"

"No, not at all; more of a compliment."

"In that case, thank you."

"You're welcome."

"Let me light that up."

"Here, do you."

"I have something for you," she said, going back to her bedroom, then returning wit a small box.

"It's not our anniversary, my birthday isn't until next month, so what's tha occasion?"

"Can I just give you a gift just because wit out it being a occasion?"

"Sure you can, do whatever you want."

"Just open it." I opened it to find a key.

"What does this go to?"

"My front door."

"Ha! Ha! Ha!"

"What's so funny?"

"You know I was going to give you a key to my crib, but was afraid you wouldn't want it."

"Heem, I had to ask Chas and Jade if they thought it was too soon to give it to you and guess what they both said."

"What?"

"They thought you already had one."

"Iciss, I know we've only been together for a few months but to me it feels like forever. Maybe it's because I've been liking and wanting you for so long."

"That's one more thing we have in common."

"You gonna pass that or smoke it all?"

"Here, I'm ready to eat anyway."

"You know I love you, right?"

"Excuse me?"

"Girl stop all tha bullshit; you heard me."

"I just wanted to make sure I heard you correctly."

"I said I L-O-V-E Y-O-U."

"I'm not slow, smart ass."

"I just wanted to make sure you heard me that time."

"I love you too Heem, I really do."

"Awe, now you got me blush'n all crazy."

"You so stupid."

"Well I better be going."

"Oh you not staying tha night wit me?"

"I would love to if that's what you want."

"Would I ask if it wasn't?"

"You not going to be happy til I kick ya butt," I said putting her in the head lock.

"Oh you done started something now."

"OOOOWWW I know you didn't just bite me? I got something for you."

"Ha! Ha! Ha! Ha! Ha! Ha! Ha! Ha!"

"Stop, oh my goood pleeease I'm sorry." She was laughing so hard her eyes were watering.

"Imma hurt you," she said, jumping on top of me, "now say sorry."

"Nope."

"Say sorry," she said, punching me in my side.

I tried to flip her over, but she wouldn't budge. Her nightgown came up, exposing her freshly shaven vagina.

"I need to get in tha shower."

"You know where it is."

I was feeling horny as hell and a cool shower would calm me down. Noticing his bulge, I couldn't help but smile. Long story short, that night was tha best sex I ever had.

CHAPTER 8

Tiz and Fire

Pop, Pop, Pop, Boom, Boom, Boom, Bong, Bong, Bong, Bong, Bong.

"These mafuckas done lost their minds out here."

"Hold me down, I got something for them."

Coop slid in tha house. A few seconds later. All you heard was TAT-TAT-TAT-TAT-TAT-TAT-TAT TAT-TAT-TAT-TAT-TAT-TAT-TAT-TAT TAT-TAT-TAT-TAT-TAT-TAT-TAT-TAT-TAT-TAT-TAT He didn't stop squeezing to tha whole 52-shot clip was empty and four bodies lay in tha middle of tha street. Shit was quiet as hell when tha police pulled up. I went back in tha house so they wouldn't ask me shit.

"Now that's how you lay a mafucka down," Coop said, washing his hands wit bleach.

"Where you get that SK from?"

"My peeps sold it to me for tha low. I been itching to let it off."

"That shit ain't had nothing to do wit us."

"Yes it did, them Dominican cats trying to find out who laid they people down."

"Nigga, what that got to do wit us?"

"Swish we deal wit Fresh and his peeps so that shit is our beef too."

"Do you think they would do tha same for us?"

"You must of forgot about that Santana incident."

"Nah, how could I."

"Who you think sent him to tha boneyard?"

"I thought that was ya work."

"I told you it wasn't."

"Yeah and I thought you was joking."

"Nah Fresh did that for us."

"Damn, I really thought that was you."

"Imma hit Fresh up let him know what's jumping off, here twist this up."

"Yo what tha biz Youngin'?"

"Them Dominican cats was up here on some Wild Wild West shit."

"Did anybody get hurt?"

"Yeah them."

"Huh?"

"Me and Swish was on tha porch when that shit popped off I snuck up on them and let my SK go killing four of them."

"So you finally got to use that jawn?"

"Yeah."

"Did anybody see you?"

"Nah and if they did, they didn't know it was me. I had a mask on."

"So tha other ones got away?"

"It was only those for out there."

"Keep ya eyes open it's more of 'em."

"Every time they come through they gonna get it."

"A'ight, just be careful. I can't afford yall catching no murder beef or getting knocked off."

"You ain't gotta worry about neither of those things."

"OK, I got something for you. I'll call you later."

"Yo what he say?"

"He got something for us and he wants us to be safe."

"I just got off tha phone wit my young boy Coop. He said Flacco's peoples was up there on some wild, wild West shit."

"That's probably where all those cops were rushing to."

"He said he laid four of 'em down."

"These cats gonna be a problem. They just gonna keep sending 'em down."

"Well, we just gonna keep sending them to tha boneyard."

"Fuck all that extra shit they gon' just keep coming unless we kill that nigga Flacco, which shouldn't be hard since Madi has his trust."

"That could go that way or they could just send down a whole lot of them Swala Swala mafucka's."

"Ya boy, Rell talkin' a lot of shit."

"I knew I should have just pushed his shit back."

"Hit Beefy, see if that nigga is out there."

"I doubt it since he still in a wheelchair."

"He should be in a coffin not a damn wheelchair!"

"We need to stay focused on Flacco and his peoples, Rell isn't a threat to us.'"

"Not yet anyway."

"What's that supposed to mean?"

"Never ever underestimate anybody it's tha ones you think won't pose a threat that always do."

"Hold that thought," Tiz said, answering his phone.

"Hello."

"Hey Tiz."

"Who is this?"

"It's Fire."

"You must be bored."

"Why you say that?"

"You called, I hit you wit my number a month ago."

"Boy it's only been two weeks."

"So what made you decide to call me now?"

"Truthfully, I was going thru my phone book and came across ya name."

"Damn, I feel insulted."

"It's not like that."

"How is it then?"

"I've been so busy that I just forgot."

"I know you can come up wit a better excuse than that."

"You right, I can; I didn't call because I didn't want to seem pressed."

"Now that I can believe."

"I'm sure you got plenty of broads blowing ya phone up."

"Not me."

"Yeah whatever."

"Do you have any plans for later?"

"It depends."

"On what?"

"What do you have in mind."

"Something simple, dinner and a movie."

"What time and what movie?"

"What wit all tha questions?"

"What time and what movie?"

"Dinner at 8 and tha new Freddy Krueger flick."

"You don't even know where I live."

"That's why you're gonna tell me."

"521 E. 38th St."

"Be ready by 7:30."

"How should I dress?"

"Like you would if you were going to dinner and tha movies."

"I see we gonna be going at it wit that mouth of yours."

"Just be ready at 7:30," I said, then hung up, not giving her a chance to respond.

"Damn Nigga."

"That was Shawty from tha basketball game."

"Oh, that chick Fire?"

"That's the one."

"I thought you was taking homegirl to tha movies tonight?"

"Not no more, I'm bout to tell her something came up."

"You got too many broads you need to settle down."

"Now why would I do some dumb shit like that when I can have my cake and eat it too."

"I use to think like til I met Turk."

"If I could find a broad like all you Niggaz got, I might consider it."

"I gotta pick Turk up her car is in tha shop. Imma hit you up later."

"You know my number."

"Bre are you dropping Zia off at my moms?"

"Ms. Sady probably doesn't want to be bothered tonight."

"She called me and said that AJ was coming over and for me to bring Zia over also."

"Well, then, I guess we can drop her off on our way to Jade's and Ahmad's."

"Oh yeah, I almost forgot they did invite us over for dinner."

"Is that ya phone or mines?"

"Yours, my phone is right here."

She went upstairs to answer her phone, so I took out my phone to call Fresh back."

"What up Big Homey?"

"You know me, just doing tha family thing and deening."

"That's what's up, I hadn't heard from you in a minute so I thought it was only right for me to call you."

"Funny cause last night when Bre was on tha phone wit Turk. I said I would call you today, but you beat me to it."

"I'm pretty sure Ahmad has told you about tha situation wit these Dominican cats."

"Yeah he has. He also told me that yall have it under control."

"Every time we kill a few of them, they just send more; I told him we need to off tha head nigga."

"I don't think that would be wise."

"That's the same thing Heem said."

"He was taught by tha best so it doesn't surprise me he would say that. You see, Fresh if you do kill this guy 9 outta 10 his peoples will rise tha body count of tha whole city, not just on tha hill. And if they do that it, makes it hard to make money wit police runnin' around all crazy."

"So we're suppose to just keep shooting out wit these cats?"

"As crazy as this may sound, yes because they'll get tired before you will."

"Imma let you go, but I will stay in touch."

After I hung up wit Maze I thought about everything he said.

"Asalamu Alaikum."

"Wailakum Salam."

"You OK?"

"Yeah, I'm fine I just hope Fresh, Killer, Tiz, and Heem will be."

"What's going on?"

"Nothing you need to be concerned wit."

"If it concerns you, it concerns me!"

"Come on let's pick Zia up from daycare so we can take her to tha park for a little while before we drop her off."

"Killer I want you to be safe."

"Lexis what I tell you bout worrying?"

"I'm sorry I can't help it I be scared for you."

"You know I can take care of myself in tha streets."

"I know but I still be worried."

"Any time you get or feel worried pick up tha phone and call me."

"I just don't know what, we would do if something happens to you."

"Who's we?"

"Me and your child."

"My child, you're pregnant?"

"Yes, I just found out a few days ago."

"Why didn't you tell me?"

"Because you already had a lot on ya mind."

"Fuck that Lexis, you being pregnant is more important than anything else. So how far are you and do you plan on keeping it?"

"I'm only five weeks and if you want me to get rid."

"Hell no!"

"You didn't even let me finish."

"I don't believe in that shit."

"Good cause I wasn't doing that anyway."

"So why, never mind."

"You couldn't answer your own question."

"You is a funny chick."

"That's why you love me."

"Who told you that?"

"Oh you don't love me?"

"Of course I do boo-boo."

"Unh huh, now come give me a kiss before you leave."

"Wow that was one hell of a kiss."

"I know."

"Lexis."

"Yes."

"I want a son."

"Me too, see you when you get back in."

I had to call all tha fellas to tell 'em tha good news.

"Man I already knew. You forgot that's my cousin?"

"How come you didn't tell me Heem?"

"She made me swear on my Nana that I wouldn't."

"Who else knows?"

"I think Fresh."

"You Niggaz could've told me."

"We felt it was her job to tell you, not ours."

"You right, I ain't mad at yall."

"I know you happy."

"Damn right I am, this is my first seed. I was starting to think I couldn't have kids."

"You finally stop shooting blanks."

"Fuck you Nigga."

"Where are you at?"

"On my way to tha supermarket to pick up a few things."

"Iciss got you on a mission."

"Naw, I was going to cook tonight."

"You cook?"

"Nigga I cook better than tha average woman."

"You would be surprised; ask ya girl."

"Did Fresh tell you we playing ball tomorrow?"

"Yeah, he told me earlier."

"Him and Tiz wanna play us for tha money."

"That's not a fair game."

"I tried to tell them that."

"Hey, it's their money if they wanna lose it."

"They don't think you can ball."

"Why cause I never play when yall play?"

"Probably so, I've never seen you ball, but Lexis said you nice."

"I had a scholarship to West Virginia. I just went another route."

"Lexis told me."

"Damn, is it anything she hasn't told you?"

"She didn't say nothing about you cooking." Ha! Ha! Ha!

"Killer you a funny nigga."

"I'm just keeping it 100."

"As you should but yo let me grab this stuff. I'll hit you later."

"Nigga you know I won't hear from you til tomorrow."

"You probably right what time we ballin'?"

"Around 10 o'clock, is that too early?"

"In the words of Tupac, I'm up before tha sunrise, first to hit tha block."

"I heard that, I might as well go back to the crib."

"Don't tell Lexis I knew either."

"Come on, you know me better than that."

"I know that's why I said don't tell her, I knew."

All he could do was laugh because he knew I knew he was going to say something to her, about me knowing.

"I'll holla."

"Hello."

"I'm out front."

"Here I come."

When Fire came out my mouth dropped open.

"You better close ya mouth before something flies in it."

"You look good."

"Minus tha sling."

"It might be my shit but tha sling makes you look even sexier."

"Flattery will get you nowhere."

"Flattery no, truth yeah."

"Anyway I like ya 750."

"I don't know if I should consider that an insult or a joke."

"What do you mean by that?"

"This a 850."

"My bag, what's tha difference though?"

"About 30 to 40 grand."

"I didn't know my bag."

"I hope you don't mind if we go to tha movies first."

"Whatever you wanna do."

"Freddy still that dude."

"It was a good movie."

"How would you know you was too busy putting ya face into my arm."

"Shut up."

"I hope you like steak."

"Like steak, boy pleeeease what Black person doesn't."

I pulled up to Texas Roadhouse and it was kind of packed.

"Which one of my girls did you talk to?"

"Huh?"

"I know you had to talk to one of 'em."

"Why is that?"

"This is my favorite restaurant."

"Mines too. At least I know we have one thing in common."

"Are you sure you didn't talk to Des or Val?"

"Positive."

"Well, then I guess we do have one thing in common."

"I don't know about you but I'm starving like a Ethiopian."

"So am I and are ready know what I want; tha steak, shrimp and crab cake dinner."

"Now that's two things we have in common; that's all I eat."

"I know you talk to Des or Val now."

"Call 'em."

"What?"

"Call 'em."

"I am," she said pulling out her iPhone.

"Hello."

"Hey Val, did you talk to Tiz today? Oh, do you know if Val did? Is she, put her on, did you talk to Tiz? No because he took me to dinner at my favorite spot and ordered tha same meal I always get. Well, I'll call yall after my date. Bye."

"Apology accepted."

"I'm sorry, I should have believed you."

"Fire you'll learn that I am honest. If you want to know something just ask, I'll tell you."

"In that case, do you have a girl?"

"Nah, just friends."

"Why not?"

"I haven't found tha right one yet. What about you?"

"All guys want one thing and one thing only."

"What would that be?"

"Sex, Sex, Sex!"

"So why did you come out wit me then?"

"To see where ya head is."

"I could be wrong and this is just an assumption but I believe it's on my shoulders."

"You're a comedian too, wow."

"You can't be serious all tha time."

"Trust me, I know."

After we finished dinner, I drove by Fire back to her house where we sat in my car and talked for about an hour.

"You seem like a up and up guy."

"Maybe just maybe because I am."

"If I was to ask you to come in would you think you was getting some?"

"Do you want tha truth?"

"Of course I do."

"If you were to invite me in, I wouldn't try nothing."

"Yeah right."

"Let me finish."

"I'm listening."

"I wouldn't try but if you came on to me I would knock you down and not call no more. Reason being if you let me hit on the first night how many other Niggaz done did tha same."

"But what if I was just really feeling you?"

"I still have the ask how many other Niggaz you was really feeling?" I had to admit he was definitely game tight if nothing else.

"You know what to say."

"Maybe you didn't hear me earlier when I said I don't lie!"

"I did hear you."

"So why are you trying to play me then? "

"Boy ain't nobody trying to play you."

"Well, I'm bout to be out; hit my phone if you want to hang out again."

"Did I scare you off."

"Nah, I'm just being respectful," I said looking at my watch.

"I'm grown, I don't have no curfew, besides it's only 11:32."

"Oh My Bag." Des and Val pulled up.

"Hey bitch, you still on ya date?"

"What it look like?"

We on our way to Philly."

"Go ahead, I'll holla at you."

You don't want to go wit us?"

"I follow yall."

"Can I ride wit you or you rolling dolo?"

"That's up to you."

"Des."

"What's up?"

"We goin to follow yall."

"Do yall want to go to Plush or Palmers?" Fire looked at me.

"Let's hit Samba's."

"Where is that?"

"7th & Girard, they stay open til 4 in tha morning."

"Tiz said we should hit Samba."

"Where tha hell is that?"

"Just follow us but hold on let me run in and use tha bathroom."

"Hold on, I need to go too." I rolled up 2 Dutches while she did that.

"Do you mind if I get in?"

"Nah."

"You got some of that for sale?"

"Here, you ain't gotta buy it."

"Thank you, my girl really likes you, so don't hurt her or you gonna have to deal wit me."

"She seems like good folk."

"She is. Does this club be jumpin'?"

"Yeah, I hope you can drive because I be rolling."

"I'm like tha Black Danaca Patrick." Ha! Ha! Ha!

"What we miss?"

"Not much. He asked if I could drive."

"You have no ideal."

"I hope yall don't mind if I stop at tha Highway Inn first?"

"Nope 'cause I was going to tell you to swing by there so I could get something for the ride and some Dutches."

"I already got Dutches."

"I only smoke Dro."

"Dro, that shit played out wit tha whop."

"You crazy," Val said walking back to Des car.

"Smoke that shit I gave Des and I bet you a bean you change ya mind."

"Will see. What kind of weed you smoke?"

"Tha best."

"I heard that." Highway Inn was packed as always.

"What yall drinking?"

"I drink Goose but they drink Patron," she said pulling her money out.

"Don't disrespect me, put ya money away. Come on yall. I got yall Fire already told me what yall drink."

"We need some pineapple juice and Dutches."

"You can't smoke what I gave you in no Dutch you got a put that in a Purple Haze Wrap. I'll be right back."

"Girl you better not fuck this up. I know because he is feeling you. And tha fact he got money is a bonus."

"I don't need his money."

"Maybe not but it won't hurt."

"Tiz what up Big Homey?"

"Bones what's good?"

"Same shit, on my way back to tha trap."

"Always on tha grind."

"Gotta make sure this paper is right."

"I definitely feel you."

"Yo let me get two pints of Patron, a pint of Grey Goose, a pint of Bombay, 3 pineapples, a orange juice, 5 wrap, and 4 packs of doublemint."

"Damn where tha party at?"

"I'm on my way up top."

"Is that Fire, Val and Des wit you?"

"Yeah."

"Which one you hitting?"

"None."

"Well, which one you wit?"

"Fire."

"Man good luck wit that."

"Why you say that?"

"Do you know how many Niggaz tried to hit that with no success?"

That's good, I ain't gotta worry about nobody saying they hit it once I get her."

"Yeah, good luck trying."

"I hear you."

"Now Val that's my old thing."

"What up yall," Bones said walking back to his whip."

I caught Val rolling her eyes.

"Imma hit you in tha a.m."

I gave them their stuff then got in my car.

"How you know bones?"

"That's my peoples."

"He use to mess wit Val til she caught him creeping."

"She still wants him."

"How you know?"

"I just do, trust me."

I took a mental note to ask her later. I mixed my drink, rolled 2 wraps, and put on Lil' Baby CD in and hit tha highway.

CHAPTER 9

Give Love Another Chance

"Flacco these guys are a real problem. We've lost too many men already. I think we need to illuminate the whole city until somebody starts talking."

"I thought that's what you been doing?"

"Only tha West Side."

"I think we need to cut our losses and move on; it's not like tha spot was generating a lot of money."

"Fuck tha money when they killed Dominic, Juan, and Jose it came personal for me!"

"Do you think it was those guys who you were dealing wit?"

"At first I did but why would they take tha money and drugs?"

"To make it look like a robbery."

"My female friend knows people who gave her a few names, but nobody will talk."

"I have an old friend, let me see if I can discreetly find out anything."

"OK."

"I'll call you in a few days but til then lay low."

"Hey Papi."

"Hey Madi."

"You OK?"

"Yeah, I just have a lot on my mind right now."

"Maybe I can help," she said, unzipping my zipper. Before I could protest, she had me in her warm mouth. "Umm, OOO, Oh Yeeees, Mama!"

"You like that Papi?"

"Yes." As soon as she put my whole penis in her mouth and massage my balls, I felt myself about to cum.

"Mama I'm bout to cum."

"Cum for me Papi, cum for me." 3 seconds later, I was releasing myself inside her mouth.

"Don't worry Papi I clean you up," she said, doing just that wit her tongue.

"I really needed that."

"Madi, have you heard anything else about tha killings?"

"No, just what I already told you that they said it was Chad and Boom."

"Do you know them?"

"No, I never heard of them, they said they from out Claymont somewhere."

"Do ya peoples know what they look like?"

"I don't know but I can find out when I go in town later."

"I'd appreciate it."

"Anything for you Papi."

I could tell Flacco had feelings for me, but for me, it was all about tha money, no strings attached. I've been down this road so many times I don't let myself fall in love wit my mark. I remember one time when I did catch feelings and it almost got me killed, so I promised myself I would never catch feelings for any of my marks again. I mean who wouldn't fall for a guy who wines and dines you 24/7? I made a mistake but lesson learned.

"Papi, did you talk to your people?"

"Yes, he say he has a friend down here that might be able to help out."

"Well, that's a good thing, right?"

"I suppose but I don't think he'll say anything if he knows anything at all."

"You're probably right; I'll see what I can find out."

"Thank you you've been very helpful."

"That's what I do for people I care about."

"Hello my friend."

"What's up Milan is there a problem wit my brother?"

"No, I actually heard that you have a situation on ya hands could I be of some assistance?"

"That's news to me; I wasn't aware of any situation. Maybe you can enlighten me."

"As you know, I have a few contacts in Wilmington."

"Yeah and."

"And they called me to see if I had any of my peeps down there. When I told them I didn't they let me know that there were some Dominicans trying to take over some of your territory."

"Milan I'm no longer in tha biz-ness, so I don't have any territory."

"Then perhaps they meant Heem."

"I don't think so; he never said anything about it and I'm certain he would've mentioned something like that."

"Yeah, I guess so. I just wanted to see if you needed me to send some help ya way?"

"Nah, my brother doesn't have anything to do wit whatever is going on wit that."

"OK."

"None of ya people are involved right?"

"Nah, well that's all I called for." After hanging up, I played tha conversation back that I just had wit Milan. Something wasn't right but I didn't and couldn't put my finger on it at that moment.

"Asalamu Alaikum."

"Wailakum Salam."

"I called you over to holla at you bout that situation wit them Dominican cats."

"What about it?"

"I'm not sure but I think they might be tied in wit Milan."

"What makes you say that?"

"He called me talking about he heard through his contacts I had a situation; then he started asking questions."

"I still don't see how that ties him and wit them cats."

"I just got a feeling and normally I'm right when I get a feeling about something."

"So what do you want to do?"

"Just have Sly find out what's going on wit Milan and we'll go from there."

"So you coming out of retirement?"

"Nah, I'm just makin' sure Heem and tha fellas are a'ight."

"Sly's gonna love this because he just called and said he was bored and thinkin' about getting back in."

"Well, this will give him something to do for a while. How is Zia I haven't seen her since we went to dinner that night?"

"She's 3 going on 20."

"I heard that. I need to go see about this building I'm trying to buy, so I'll hit Sly and give you a call later."

"Aye Rell, you'll never guess who I saw wit ya peeps tha other night up Philly."

"Who my peeps?"

"Fire."

"Fuck that stuck up bitch!"

"You wasn't saying that when you was spending that money on her."

"That's cause I was trying to hit it."

"Nigga I told you I don't know nobody that has hit that and a lot have tried."

"Well, who my peeps?"

"Tha boy Tiz."

"Fuck him too, he sided wit that bitch ass nigga Killer."

"That's his boy; what do you expect?"

"For him to stay neutral, since he fuck wit both of us."

"On some real shit that's like me choosing Lap over you and I fuck wit both of yall."

"But you be wit me all day every day."

"My point exactly."

"I feel you."

"Damn just spoke her up," he said pointing at Fire who was getting out of her car in front of Kennedy Fried."

"Watch this."

"Where are you going?"

"To throw salt on a wound."

"Girl don't look now, but here comes Rell."

"See that's exactly why we should've went to tha one on 30th; I'm not for his dumb shit today."

"Damn Fire, I see you still looking good as hell. My man must be playing his part."

"Excuse me."

"I said, my man must be playing his part."

"Who's ya man?"

"Come on Shawty you know damn well who I'm talkin' bout."

"No I don't."

"Well, you should tell Tiz to keep quiet."

Tha look on her face said it all.

"At least now I know you not butch."

"And what's that supposed to mean?"

"He told me ya shot was off tha meter and tha head is ridiculous."

"Yeah, whatever Nigga."

"Hey, don't be mad at me; I ain't say it. I'm just glad my peeps got to hit it."

"For your info ya peeps ain't hit shit!"

"Save that shit, he not going to lie on his wood."

"Well, he is," she said, snatching her bag and storming out.

"I can't believe that mafucka lied like that."

"Rell probably tha one lying."

"How would he know I was even talking to Tiz if he didn't tell him we were?"

"Oh yeah, I didn't think about that."

"I'm bout to call his ass up right now."

I called twice but got no answer neither time. I was too pissed to leave a message on his machine.

"Where are you going? I thought we were going to Val's house?"

"We are but after I ride through Madison Street."

"He got you pissed off."

"You damn right and to think I was really feeling him."

When we got by tha park I spotted him talking to tha same dude he was wit that day at tha game.

"There he go Fire."

"I see him," I said pulling over then jumping out.

"Hey Shawty."

"Mafucka don't hey shawty me."

"Whoa Whoa slow ya roll."

"Fuck you! Why would you lie and say you fucked me and I gave you head?"

"Huh, what you talkin' bout?"

"You know exactly what she talkin' bout," Des said in Fire's defense.

"Nah, I don't."

"What tha fuck ever. You can lose my number."

"Hold up Shawty who told you some bullshit like that?"

"Ya man."

"My man who?"

"Rell."

"Rell?"

"Yeah Rell from tha Ave."

"He didn't say no dumb shit like that."

"Yes he did and I know he not lying. Cause how did he even know we was talkin'?"

"I don't know but I don't even fuck wit dude like that no more since my peoples shot him."

"Not according to him."

"You believe that nigga over me."

"Why would he lie?"

"He must like you."

"Lose my number."

"Normally, I'd be like fuck you and keep it moving, but Imma prove it to you." He pulled out his phone and punched in a number after a few rings, Rell picked up.

"Yo player." He put it on speaker so we could all hear.

"What tha fuck is up wit you Nigga?"

"Come again."

"Keep my name out of ya Fuckin' mouth or we gon' have a problem!"

"Fuck you talkin' bout?"

"Fire just left from over here snappin' cause you lied to her."

"Man I was just fuckin' wit that bitch I didn't know she was gonna run tell you."

"You told her I said I hit and got some head. Why wouldn't she?"

"Damn Nigga you called like that's ya bitch or something."

"She is my girl, so watch ya mouth."

"Fuck you and that bitch if that's how you feel!"

"Didn't you just get out of a wheelchair for runnin' ya gums?"

"You heard what I said."

"Tell ya family to make funeral arrangements cause you a dead man walkin'." After hearing that, I felt bad for snapping on him tha way I did.

"I owe you an apology."

"Nah that goes back to what I said, I don't lie Shawty."

"I just thought since nobody knew we were talkin' he had to be telling tha truth."

"One of his boys probably seen us out."

"Oh shit!"

"What girl?"

"Tha boy that was wit him was at Samba tha night we were."

"That explains how he knew cause yall was all over each other."

"I really owe you an apology. I'm so sorry."

"You can make it up to me at dinner tonight."

"You got that."

"Come on Des."

"Sorry Tiz but that's my girl you know how it goes."

"It's cool, you suppose to ride out wit ya girl. If you didn't, I would question ya loyalty to her."

"Bitch, I feel real dumb."

"I don't know why? You did what anybody would have done. Like he said, I'm going to ride out wit you, but I didn't think he would do no shit like that. If he does something to Rell, we could get conspiracy."

"We are not going to get shit cause we didn't hear nothing."

"I know what I did hear him say."

"What?"

"That you was his girl."

"I heard that, but since he said we left, I did not say anything."

"Bitch you didn't say nothing cause you wanna be."

"Pleeeease."

"You do."

"Whatever."

"So you saying you don't?"

"I never said that but we only been talking for a couple weeks."

"And what that mean?"

When she didn't answer she said that's what I thought.

"All I'm saying is, would it be a bad thing if you were?"

"I don't know if I'm really ready for a relationship."

"Girl ever since James cheated you been avoiding relationships. I think it's time to give it another shot."

"Yeah, you're probably right."

"Damn, what ya have to do catch tha chicken?"

"Girl no we ran into Rell who tried to get all this stuff started with Tiz."

"What stuff?"

"He said Tiz told him he knocked Fire off and she gave him head."

"Stop lying."

"She's not lying."

"I know you called Tiz?"

"Yeah but he didn't answer."

"I can't wait to see his lying ass so I can tell him off."

"No need, we found him in tha park on Madison Street."

"So what did he say? No wait don't tell me, he denied it and to think I actually thought he'd be good for you."

"Yeah, he denied it, Fire told him to fuck off and lose her number."

"That's good."

"Then he told her he would normally tell her to keep it moving, but he pulled his phone out and called Rell."

"He was probably faking like he was talking to him."

"No he put his phone on speaker."

"So you heard Rell say it again?"

"No we heard Tiz snap on him and Rell said he was just messing wit Fire."

"Hold up, so you're telling me Rell's bitch ass lied."

"Yup."

"What was tha purpose of that?"

"His boy seen us together at tha club and probably told Rell."

"And Rell got jealous then went into hate mode."

"Bingo."

"Just think, I was ready to feed him to tha wolves."

"Don't feel bad, I did tha same thing only to his face then had to apologize."

"I felt really bad tha way I cussed him out."

"So yall still talkin' then, right?"

"Oh I forgot he told Rell Fire was his girl."

"She went from cussing him out to be in his girl."

"No, I went from cussing him out to going out to dinner wit him tonight."

"You might as well be his girl not like, you got anything else to do."

"Fuck you bitch!"

"I tried to tell her tha same thing that she needs to give love another chance."

"If it will keep yall off my back, I'll consider it."

CHAPTER 10

Tha Game

"Yo, what the biz is?"

"Hello my friend, I'm ready to see you."

"A'ight, give me two hours."

"Same place this time make it 30."

"No problem."

"Milan why do you continue to do biz-ness wit those people?"

"Tha work is tha best on tha East Coast and tha price is affordable."

"You don't think they had nothing to do wit what happen to Flacco's boys in tha ones we sent down?"

"No, I tried to find out through Ahmad but he said that it wasn't his brother who was beefing wit 'em."

"I think Flacco needs to come back up."

"I told him tha same thing, but he's not trying to hear it."

"You busy?"

"Nah."

"I need you to take that ride wit me."

"I am in tha park, come scoop me."

"Be there in 30 minutes."

I pulled up at tha same time Turk was droppin' Fresh off.

"What it do Big Homie?"

"Ya guess is better than mines."

"I haven't seen ya boy Flacco, he flying under tha radar."

"He think he is, he's just laying low for a while."

"How you know all that?"

"You forgot Madi on tha job."

"Oh shit I did. Well, actually I thought she was back in B-More."

"Nah, as soon as she finds out who his supplier is, she's gon' to take him out back and put him under."

"She must be falling off 'cause it's been a few months and she still don't know shit yet."

"It's not that she's falling off tha nigga just cautious."

"I would too if your Niggaz got killed."

"You don't have to worry about that."

"Yall gonna be here?"

"Yeah, we ain't going nowhere. We gotta meet Milan."

"Heem I don't trust that mafucka."

"He cool or Ahmad wouldn't have turned us on."

"Yeah, but he might not know that nigga is a snake."

"Heem, people change."

"All I'm saying is be careful."

"I always do Fresh."

On tha ride to meet Milan, I tried to think if he ever did anything suspicious that I may have overlooked at tha time but couldn't think of anything.

"Killer park on tha other side this time."

"Why, what's up?"

"I just need to see something, that's all.

I spotted two guys in a black Taurus pulling up. I could tell they were not there to get a room by their body language.

"You picked up on that too, huh?"

"Yeah."

"Do you think they Fed?"

"Nah, Milan's people."

"Why would they park around here and not on tha other side like they always do?"

"Simple he's been coming wit extra men tha whole time."

I pulled out and drove back to tha other side where Milan was already waiting.

"We gonna do it a little different this time," I said getting out tha car.

"Is everything good my friend?"

"Yes, I'm just going inside to have a quick drink; won't you join me."

"It's too early to drink."

"It's never too early to drink, have ya man put tha money in my car then join us."

He motioned for his man to put tha money in tha car; once he did, I locked tha doors wit my alarm.

"So, my friend, what's this really about?" I wanted to see if I could really trust him.

"There's a black Taurus wit two men inside on tha other side of tha building. I think they are Feds."

"Are you sure of this my friend?"

"I saw them drive in and position their selves where they could see us. That's why I didn't pull in our usual spot."

Killer looked at me like what are you doing.

"I don't think that they are Feds."

"What makes you so sure?"

"If they were for tha minute we got out they would've been all over us."

"OK," I said, handing him tha room key.

"I better be heading back. I have some other people waiting on me."

"A'ight my friend. I'll call you when I'm ready."

As soon as we got into tha car, Killer ask me what that was about.

"Tha nigga lied and said he didn't know who they were."

"Maybe he really didn't. Where are you going now?"

We switched cars wit my young boy then sat there until Milan came out.

"Snake ass Nigga! I don't know what his agenda is but I do know he can't be trusted."

"Why wouldn't he just say they were wit him?" Killer asked as we watched Milan talk to tha two guys that were in tha black Taurus.

"I think you should call Ahmad and see what his take is on it."

"Yeah, you're right," I said pulling out my phone.

"Asalamu Alaikum."

"Wailakum Salam."

"What's tha deal wit Milan?"

"What do you mean?"

"I told him about what just transpired and how he lied."

"Heem I don't know; tha other day he call me trying to get some info."

"Info on what?"

"I don't really know."

"Why you ain't let me know?"

"Because I got sly on him. Imma just stop dealing wit tha nigga; it's not like I need his money."

"That's up to you, but you know I support you no matter what."

"I know you do Big Homey."

"Iciss tells me you two are thinking about moving in together."

"Yeah, she said something about it."

"Well, Jade is cooking a big dinner on Sunday."

"You know we'll be there."

"A'ight Asalamu Alaikum."

"Wailakum Salam." (Click)

"What he say?"

"Just that he has sly on him to see what he's really up to."

"I say we say fuck him and keep it moving."

"It's already a done deal."

"That's all it is then."

"I forgot all about tha game today."

"Who's playing?"

"We play Northside, winner plays C.B.W for tha chip. Fuck!"

"What's up?"

"Josh just text me, he's not going to be able to play he sprained his ankle."

"Yall should be a'ight wit out him."

"Man wit out him we can't win."

"Yall got a nice squad, he's not tha team."

"Hold up, that's Fresh, hello."

"Yo Josh hit my phone and said he messed his ankle up and can't play."

"I know; he sent me a text."

"Tha game starts in less than an hour what we gon' do?"

He looked at me and said, "We can use Heem; remember we had him on tha roster."

"That nigga can't ball that's why he's always coming up wit an excuse every time we 'posed to play."

"Hey what other option do we have?"

"OK just make sure yall on time."

"Man, I ain't playing no ball today."

"We need you."

"Too bad."

"You always talking like you can ball and I always go to bat for you and I never seen you play before. I starting to think you can't ball and that's why you never play wit us."

"Ha! Ha! Ha! Yo you a funny dude, I see what you trying to do and it's not going to work."

"Hey Man, you don't have to play we just need you on tha bench to fill tha 7-man roster."

"Nigga if I suit up, I'm not sitting on nobody sideline lookin' like a fool."

"That's up to you."

After I dropped Killer off I shot to Iciss so I could put my gear on.

"Where you going?"

"I just let Killer talk me into playing in this game tonight."

"Good."

"Good?"

"Yeah, now I have somebody to cheer for Chas, Lexis, Turk, Bre and Jade are going to tha game."

"Do you know if Ahmad and Maze are going?"

"I think so." My phone went off.

"Hello."

"Hey, do you still have ya black LeBron's?"

"Of course."

"Bring 'em, we got everything else for you."

"A'ight, I'm on my way."

When I walked outside, Jade was pulling up.

"Asalamu Alaikum."

"Wailakum Salam."

"Hey Cuz, I heard you playing in tha championship game."

"This ain't for tha chip."

"Yes it is."

"Killer said…"

"He just wanted you to play."

"Imma hurt that nigga."

"Just don't tell him I told you."

"Where is ya slow ass girl?"

"Don't be rushing me, yall know I just got off a little while ago."

"Well, hurry up tha game starts in 45 minutes and we want good seats."

"We thought you change ya mind. Here you go, change into this."

They all had on black shorts and shirts wit their number airbrushed on them. They were already warming up when I came back. Josh was on tha sideline wit his crutches.

"Heem shoot a couple jumpers to warm up."

"I don't need to shoot no jumpers, I'm already warmed up," I said walking to tha sideline to holla at Josh.

"Yo that nigga can't ball and he's not getting into tha game."

"Well you Niggaz better not get in no foul trouble."

Tha buzzer went off to start tha game Tiz put Jam in instead of me but I didn't say nothing. Three minutes into tha game Jam got into foul trouble so Tiz put Cameron in.

"Cameron stay wit ya man there's no way he should be blowing by you like that."

"Tell him to play him to his left he can't go right."

"Cameron play him to his left."

"What tha fuck, time out, time out."

The ref blew his whistle to let them know we called time out. "What tha fuck are yall doing out there? Yall gotta play. defense, it's only tha first quarter and we down 10."

"Cameron, you gotta play ya man to his left. Fresh and Killer yall gotta call tha pics out."

"You know a lot for a nigga that can't ball," Fresh said wit an attitude.

"One thing for sure, two things for certain if I was playing we wouldn't be losing."

"Well, get ya ass in tha game then."

"I'll play in tha second quarter."

"I told you he can't play no damn ball," Tiz said wit a smile.

Tha ref blew tha whistle to let us know our time was up. I looked over at Lexis, who gave me a look that said, get ya ass in tha game. At tha end of tha first, C.B.W. what's up 15.

"They ain't giving us no calls."

"You Niggaz playing soft and I'm telling yall right now. If you not gon' go hard wit me stay on tha sideline," I said, walking on tha court.

"Heem, you can't play no ball!" tha young boy Var yelled.

"I bet we win."

"Put ya money where ya mouth is then."

I walk over to him, "How much you want to bet?"

"Bet a stack."

"Bet two Nigga!"

"It's a bet."

Killer passed me tha ball I dribbled up court runnin' tha point. The boy Medz tried to rip me, I hit him wit a mean cross, went down tha lane and banged it on Chris. The whole gym went crazy. I just looked at Fresh and winked.

"Trap, Trap," I yelled, forcing a turnover.

Fresh hit me in tha corner and I knocked down a three. We continued to trap, forcing two more turnovers cutting tha game to six. C.B.W. called a timeout.

"Listen, we gon' go wit tha 2-1-2."

"Tha trap is working."

"Yeah, but they gon' be expecting it, so we switch up on 'em. We got this game, trust me."

"Yo Nigga, you got game like Kobe."

"Come on so we can take this game over."

For tha next 5 minutes, it was all Heem. He was knocking down 3's like they were layups. He ended tha half wit a fast break 360 dunk that sent tha gym into a frenzy.

"All this time, we really thought you couldn't ball."

"I told you if I didn't catch that case, I would've probably went into the league."

"Nigga we thought you was just talking to be talking."

"Listen, tha second half they gonna be trying to double me so that should leave one of yall open. Just keep playing hard and we got this in tha bag. We hold 4, so don't let up on 3 defense."

"3 defense!" we all yelled.

We picked up where we left off and just like I said, they double-teamed me, leaving Killer open to knock down tha three. The final score was 79-70 us. I finished with 29–10–10–3.

"Did I make yall believers or do you still think I can't ball?"

"Hey Baby, I would hug you, but you all sweaty."

"You don't mind when I'm all sweaty no other time."

"Shut up," Iciss said, punching me in my arm.

"I told you my Cuz was tha shit on tha court."

"Yeah, yeah."

"Heem, you still got it, I see."

"Come on Ahmad, did you think I would lose it?"

"Why did you sit out tha first quarter?"

"These Niggaz didn't think I could ball."

"He never plays wit us, that's why."

"Here you go Heem," Var said, handing me my money I just beat him for.

"Good game yall, Heem I didn't know you had it in you. Are yall going to play in tha midnight league?"

"They might not me."

"Too bad, I wanted to put a wager on it."

"Now that's a different story. How much?"

"5 grand."

"Make it 10 and it's a bet."

"Bet but if we win which we will, we get paid vice versa."

"Even one of us don't make it there?"

"Yup."

"Mafucka you broke in my crib!" Pop, Pop, Pop, Pop. We pushed tha girls back in tha Center so no one would get hit by a stray bullet.

"Stay in here til we say it's safe to come out."

"If they shooting why are yall going out there?"

When we walked out tha Center somebody was laying on tha ground shot.

"Hey Spank come here. Did yall see that shit?"

"Nah, who was doing tha shooting?"

"Quick hit tha boy John-John cause he hit his crib last week for a couple ones."

"Ain't John-John ya man?"

"Yeah we was coming up tha street when we spotted him coming down tha Center steps."

"Y'all need to be more careful next time my peoples was coming out."

"They was straight. He hit him close range, he caught all 4 shots."

By tha time tha police and tha ambulance came, he was already dead.

"Yall go ahead and get out of here."

"What was that all about?"

"Just another case of what happens when you take something that doesn't belong to you."

"We wouldn't know nothing bout that, come on ladies."

"Iciss let me holla at you for sec."

"What's up Baby?"

"Me and tha fellas are going out tonight."

"So are me, Chas and Turk."

"If you don't mind me asking where are yall going?"

"Why so yall can stay away from there?"

"Nah."

"Probably Plush or Samba."

"I'll probably see you tonight."

"Of course you will, you have a key."

"You know what I'm talking about, stop playing."

"If I do, first round on me," she said giving me a kiss.

"I love you Heem."

"Ditto."

"Awe that's so cute; look at yall all in love."

"Shut up Lexis."

"Boy beat it."

"So I'll see you at tha club later."

"Ok."

"Yall bitches ain't tell me yall was going out tonight."

"You ain't going nowhere."

"For your information, I'm allowed to go out til I start showing."

"That won't be long," I said rubbing her belly.

"Whatever, I got at least two more months before that."

"Unless yall wanna catch another ride, yall better come on."

"Bye."

"Bye."

"Don't be rushing nobody Jade."

"Well come on then."

"Yall better go cause you know she'll leave."

"I know, that's why I hate when she drives."

CHAPTER 11

Tha Work

"Yo son, do y'all have this shit in some weight?"

"Depends on what you trying to get."

"What tha numbers like on tha breakdown?"

"A stack a ounce."

"Damn so yall want 36 a jawn?"

"Yup."

"That's high as shit."

"Not for this work it's not, you see how they go crazy for this shit."

"Look out, just a month ago yall was coppin' off us."

"True and yall was charging us out tha ass for that bullshit."

"We need a jawn."

"And we need 36."

"Come on son."

"It is what it is."

"You got that son."

"Give us a hour."

"Just hit my phone when you ready."

"Do you want it hard or soft?"

"Hard."

"A'ight."

"Bones call Tiz so we can re up cause after I do this up we gonna be low."

"I'm already on it."

"Damn, funny how tha pancake flips."

"I'm not giving them Niggaz no deals; they wasn't looking out for us."

"Roger that."

"Yo, we gon' really score off them Niggaz?"

"This time, then next time we gon' get 3 and just take it; fuck they gon' do to us."

"We need to find out where they getting that shit from so we can have tha plug."

"I know cause they locked it down wit that shit."

"We can probably still put something on it the way tha fiends going crazy for it."

"We definitely will find out."

"Tiz I need you."

"What's up Frog?"

"I need 3 this time."

"I'll bring 5 and just hit me back wit tha 60 grand."

"A'ight," I said, knowing we would make that off just one.

That's like us getting one for free since we get 48 off one after we cook it; then we make 96 of it easy.

"How long do you need before you ready?"

"We ready now, but can you meet me on 6 and Church this time?"

"Sure, I'll be there in 30 minutes at tha most."

"You'll see me sitting on tha steps just walk in tha crib."

"I'm bout to walk to the crib to meet Tiz."

"A'ight, Imma be right here making this paper.

By tha time I got to tha crib, open tha door Tiz was pulling up wit Fresh.

"That was fast, let me run upstairs and get tha money."

"This is a nice spot."

"Me and Bones share this."

"I thought that was your spot on Bennett?"

"Yeah our trap house, we don't rest there."

"I heard that."

"You know them N.Y. cats wanna cop of us now."

"Keep an eye on them Niggaz I don't trust them."

"Me either, but they can try some funny shit if they want they'll be in for a rude awakening."

"You know we got ya back if need be."

"That's what's up."

"Be safe, I gotta handle some other shit."

"I'll hit you when I'm ready. Oh yeah, that's a 115 grand owe you 50 on tha next one."

"You and Bone need to put a team together so yall don't have to be out there all tha time."

"We two steps ahead of you we bout to have it organized like a Philly block."

"Just make sure you watch them N.Y Niggaz every time you serve them have somebody watch ya back."

"No doubt, I know they pissed that we took over but they lucky we even letting them get at a dollar around there."

I tucked 3 and took tha other 2 back up to tha block so I could do them up.

"Bone when I finish this last 9 call them Niggaz up. We not doing no biz-ness here."

"I know, we gon' have them meet us somewhere else secluded."

"Why secluded?"

"So if we have to kill them there won't be any witnesses."

"I'm bout to call them now. Where do you want them to meet us?"

"Have 'em meet us in back of Shortlidge School."

"Yo they just called, they said meet them in back of Shortlidge."

"Is that tha school right off 18th & Market?"

"Yup."

"Why they can't just bring it to us?"

"I think tha spot they getting it from is probably close to there."

"I did not think about that."

"I told you, this one is on us, next one will be on them."

"I never liked them young arrogant Niggaz anyway."

"You don't have to like a person to take their money; always remember that. Come on lets head over that way."

I parked on 17th Street while Bones slid on tha side of this building. After 15 minutes Quick pulled up wit Jas riding shotgun. I blinked tha lights to let them know I was parked behind them. I thought it was kind of strange that they both got out but I wasn't worried because Bones had tha drop on them.

"Took you Niggaz long enough."

"We had to pick up tha money."

"Next time have that shit on deck."

"You got tha work?"

"Do you got my money?"

I could tell Jas wanted to say something but I guess his better judgment told him not to. "Our next go round we are going to need 3, can we get a deal?"

"35 apiece."

"Damn, that's only a stack of each one."

"Hey man, you know how it goes."

"You rough little Nigga."

"I gotta go so just hit me."

"I'll hit you up."

Bones waited til they were gone before he came out.

"That nigga Jas gonna make me push his wig back."

"I never did like that nigga I can see right through him."

"I was wondering why they both got out to come holla at you."

"Funny, I was thinking tha same thing but I knew you had tha drop on them."

"They wouldn't know what hit 'em til it was too late."

"So did you enjoy ya dinner date last night?"

"Girl you won't believe what he did."

"Do tell."

"He rented a yacht, took me out to tha middle of nowhere. He had a live band play while we ate dinner."

"Wow sounds like you really had a beautiful night."

"Des it was tha best night of my life and he didn't even try to have sex wit me. We must of stayed out til tha sun start coming up. Then he took me home."

"I need a man like that in my life."

"He suppose to pick me up in an hour so we can get something to wear for Doc B's party next weekend."

"Oh snap, I forgot all about tha divas vs. Don's party. I need to get something myself."

"You might as well come wit us."

"I don't want to intrude."

"You won't be, let me hit him and ask him if it's cool just to make sure. Hey, I was calling to ask if Des could ride wit us since she needs to get something too. OK, I'll see you in a little bit. I told you he wouldn't care."

"Are you sure because I really don't want to impose on yall."

"Bitch didn't I say it was OK?"

"OK OK no need to get all hostile on a Sista. Do I have time to run home?"

"For what?"

"I need to get some more money."

"Go head. If he comes before you get back I'll hit ya phone and we'll pick you up."

20 minutes later Tiz was pulling up. (Beep Beep)

"Come in!" I yelled out tha door.

"Hey."

"What up Ma where Des?"

"On her way back she went home to get some more money."

"I would've loan shark her some money."

"Yeah right."

"I would've."

"I'm talking about tha loan shark part."

"You a loan shark too?" Des asked walking in.

"No, he was talkin' bout Loansharking you some money."

"I don't do that."

"First time for everything," he said looking at me wit a smile.

"I don't know why you smiling at me? I don't do that either. I'll be broke til I get paid."

"So you mean to tell me if we were in a store and they had these shoes, you really wanted, but didn't have enough For…"

"No!"

"Hold on let me finish."

"I'm all ears."

"And you didn't have enough and I said I'll give you 100 for 125 back you wouldn't jump on it?"

"No, I would wait."

"These are tha last pair and they're not getting any more in."

"Well in that case, I suppose I would."

"Are yall done. Can we go?"

"You in a rush?"

"No but I'm ready."

"OK, we out then."

"Guess what my mama told me she hate my partners, guess why she hate 'em, though all of 'em robbers. Fuck tha cops cause all of 'em robbers. White chicks da shit cause all of 'em swallow."

"This is my song."

"What you know bout this Plies and Jeezy?"

"More than you," Des said singing word for word.

"I want to hit King of Prussia first if yall don't mind."

"You driving."

"I was just asking now give me a light."

"Is that tha same weed you gave me that night?"

"Of course, that's all I smoke."

"What kind of weed is it?"

"Sour Diesle."

"Sour who?"

"Diesle."

"You gotta turn me on to your connect."

"You looking at him."

"You got it for sale?"

"Nah but I have plenty of it."

"Sell me an ounce."

"A ounce ain't going to be cheap."

"How much 150?"

"That won't even get you a quarter."

"Well damn, how much it cost?"

"180 for a quarter, 720 for an ounce."

"Are you serious?"

"Yeah."

"Well, I don't have that much so just sell me something for 150."

"I got you when we get back."

"It's always packed up here no matter when or what time you come."

"There's a parking spot right there."

As I was pulling in, two white girls almost hit my car. Trying to take my spot.

"Dumb ass bitches!" Fire said jumping out followed by Des.

"Hold tha fuck up!"

"Did I hit your car? I'm so sorry." I got out and looked at my car for any dents.

"No you good but next time you might not be so lucky."

"Like I said, my fault."

I could see Fire was about to snap so I grabbed her hand and started walking.

"Why you grab me?"

"You had that look on your face."

"What look is that?"

"Like you was about to be a bitch down look." Ha! Ha! Ha! "She definitely was."

"No harm was done, so it was cool."

"The bitch tried to get smart or didn't yall pick up on it?"

"We did, but she wasn't worth tha trouble."

As soon as I walked in tha Gucci store, I saw these brown slip ons I just had to have.

"I like those," Des said, referring to the slip ons I picked up.

"We have these in black and tan also."

"Well, let me get all 3 pairs in a 7 ½ ."

"Damn boy you got some small feet."

"Will this be all?"

"No, but you can put them on the counter."

Fire was over in tha female section trying to decide which dress she wanted to go wit these Gucci open-toe shoes she had in her hand.

"I think they both look good wit 'em."

Des looked at tha price tag then said, "Well which one you want?" That made me look.

"Get 'em both."

"I'm not balling like you. I got just enough to get my outfit and accessories."

"Don't worry about it; this is on me."

"I can pay for my own stuff."

"I'm sure you can but not today. Now put both those dresses and shoes on tha counter wit mines."

"Des I got you too."

"I am going Christian Dior or Prada this time."

When it was all said and done I dropped close to 11 grand which was nothing.

"Tiz thank you for hooking a Sista up."

"Don't worry about it Des, It ain't bout nothing that's what I do for my peeps."

"Well, I'm glad we peeps."

"Ha! Ha! Ha!"

"Yo you keep it 100 that's why I fucks wit you."

"No you fucks wit me because I'm Fire's girl."

"Yeah that too."

"I know because if she wasn't your girl we wouldn't be having this conversation."

"We're just friends."

"You mean to tell me yall been talkin' for a minute now and yall just friends still?"

"Not my shit."

"It's not mines either."

"Both yall full of it."

"I'm telling you Des It's Fire, not me."

"Don't believe that Des."

"I just came up wit tha perfect solution, why don't yall make it official now?" We both just looked at each other and shrug our shoulders.

"Yall can keep playing this cat and mouse game if yall want."

"Heem you talked to Tiz today?"

"Yeah, he took Shawty to Philly to grab an outfit for Doc B's party next week."

"You still haven't heard from Flacco?"

"Madi said he laying low trying to find out who offed his boys."

"Coop said there haven't been any more of his peoples coming through lately."

"Tell them to stay on point because they'll probably try to catch them off guard."

"I already put them on point."

"Tha Niggaz that jump ship trying to come back on board."

"Fuck 'em we ain't selling 'em nothing and nobody that deals wit us better not. They are lucky to still be alive for their act of disloyalty."

"We both agree on that."

"Sly said that Milan is meeting wit somebody down here but he doesn't know who he is."

That didn't send any red flags since I knew he had contacts down here.

"I wish I would have seen more into it and maybe somethings could've been prevented."

"Don't worry about that. He has peoples down here that's on his payroll."

"A'ight, well I'll keep you updated as things develop."

"Make sure you tell Sly if he finds out anything to get wit us before he acts on it."

"You late, you know a already did that."

"I'll see you later at the masjid."

"For sho'."

"Asalamu Alaikum."

"Wailakum Salam."

"Daddy, are you taking me over mom-mom Sady's now?"

"Yeah, get ya bag."

"Do you mind if I ride wit you?"

"Not at all."

"Ahmad did you think about what I said?"

"Baby you say so much. What are you talkin' bout?"

"Don't play dumb, you know exactly what I'm talkin' bout."

"Are you sure you want to have another baby?"

"Yes I'm sure."

"If this is what you want then yeah we can try because AJ could use a little brother or sister."

"I'm gonna have a brother or sister?"

"Yup real soon."

"Yeeeeeeah I'm going to have a sister, I'm gonna have a sister."

"Oh, so you want a little sister, huh?"

"Yes, just like Zia."

We both looked at each other then smiled.

As soon as AJ got in my mom's house he yelled, "Mom-Mom Sady, I'm having a little sister!"

"Jade you pregnant?"

"No Mom."

"Then what is AJ talking bout?"

"Me and Ahmad are going to try to have another baby."

"We wanted to wait until AJ was at least 5."

"Daddy I'm 6," he said holding up 6 fingers.

"I know how old you are."

"Mom-Mom Sady is Zia coming over too?"

"Yeah, Bre should be on her way over now."

"Yeeeeeah Zia coming over."

"He loves himself some Brazia."

"I know. He's gonna be a good big brother. So if yall don't mind me askin' what made yall decide to have another baby?"

"I wanted a little girl and wanted AJ to have a sibling."

"You might as well since Iciss ain't having none no time soon."

"She will eventually Mom right now she has her career to think about."

"Chile please, she's been a lawyer for 6 months and she's already very successful and in high demand."

"Yeah and that's why she probably doesn't want any kids right now."

"Asalamu Alaikum," Bre said walkin' in tha house.

"Wailakum Salam."

Zia ran straight to AJ then gave him a hug.

"They act more like sister and brother than cousins."

"They sure do, don't they?"

"Jade you still going to Cow Town?"

"I forgot all about that. You have to take me back to my house so I can get some money."

"No problem."

"Baby I'll see you later."

"Ok."

"Do you want me to bring you back some of that chicken you always get?"

"Sure do."

"Maze told me to bring him some back too."

"Cause he know that chicken is tha bomb."

"I think Imma try some of this chicken today to see what all tha fuss is about."

"Me too."

"Tell 'em Mom Sady they gonna be hooked."

"Yup like a fish by a fisherman," she said holding out a $20 bill.

"What is this for?"

"Bring me back 20 dollars worth please."

"Keep ya money I got you," Ahmad told her pulling out a 50.

"I know I gotta try some now."

I decided to pay Heem a visit so I swung by Iciss's since I knew he would be there.

(Knock-Knock)

"Who is it," Iciss asked from tha other side.

"Bill collector."

"You must have tha wrong house," she said swinging tha door open.

"Ahmad why you playing, come in."

"Hey Little Sis, damn it smell good; what you cooking?"

"Beef, bacon, eggs, and pancakes are you hungry?"

"As a matter fact, I was coming to see if Heem wanted to grab a bite."

"He's not here."

"He's not?"

"No he went to get some Minute Maid fruit punch."

"Him and that fruit punch, I tell you."

"He should be on his way back though."

"Where is ya wife and son?"

"AJ is over Moms Sady's Jade went to Cow Town wit Bre."

"They didn't have to call me to see if I wanted to go."

"Jade forgot she was supposed to be going."

"It's cool cause me, Chas, Turk And Lexis shooting up top to get something for Doc B's party next weekend."

"Oh, he's having a party?"

"Yeah a Divas-VS-Don's party."

"I might as well tell you me and Jade are going to have another baby."

"Seriously when?"

"Whenever she gets pregnant."

"That's what's up, I could use a niece."

"A niece, is Jade expecting?"

"Nah not yet, Asalamu Alaikum."

"Wailakum Salam."

"Damn baby you sure you got enough?"

"I gotta make sure we don't run out."

"You tha only one that drinks it."

"So what brings you by on this beautiful morning?"

"Just came to check up on yall."

"Well, let me finish cooking so we can eat."

"How's everything going?"

"Same shit, I forgot to tell you I'm not dealing wit Milan anymore."

"Nah, you told me."

"I did?"

"Yeah, you told me about tha two dudes in tha Taurus."

"That's right I did."

"Has he hit ya phone?"

"No not since I last hollered at him."

"He'll probably be calling my phone in the next day or two."

"Heem, Milan use to be a straight up dude but if ya gut is saying, don't trust him then don't."

"Breakfast is ready."

"Umm this is good you stepped ya game up Sis."

"Hey, you know it runs in tha family."

After I was done wit my food, I let them know I would see them both later and left.

CHAPTER 12

Divas Versus Dons

"Listen, meet me at tha same spot as before."

"How long?"

"40 minutes."

"A'ight, I'll probably be by myself."

I had a funny feeling he was up to something so I decided to leave now. We parked a block away and walked down. Just as we were sliding into tha alley Quick pulled up, then let Jas out so he could hide in some bushes.

"Yo remember don't come out until after you see me get tha work."

"Nigga I know what to do."

"Don't shoot him unless you really have to. I'll be back in 15 minutes."

"I told you those mafuckas couldn't be trusted!"

"Bones why do you think I came here early?"

"Stay here," Bone said sliding around tha other side of tha street. I watched as Bones eased up behind Jas wit out so much as a sound.

"If you even think about reaching for your strap, Imma put ya brains all over these bushes. Don't even turn around."

I hit him in tha back of his head wit tha butt of my gun, then pulled his from tha small of his back.

"Now turn ya bitch ass over. Why would you be hiding in tha bushes where Frogs is suppose to meet Quick?"

"Just to make sure yall wasn't on no funny shit."

"Nigga I heard Quick tell you not to come out til he had tha work and not to kill him unless necessary."

"Well, if you heard him, why are you askin' me?"

"You know what?"

"What?"

Pit, Pit, Pit, 3 shots in tha chest; he was shaking, so I put one in tha middle of his forehead to make sure he was dead. When I stepped out from the bushes Frog was pulling up.

"Come on get in. He's no longer a problem to or for us, what about Quick?"

"Yo, I'm not going to be able to meet you right now."

"Is everything OK?"

"My folks where I keep tha work don't get off until 9 o'clock."

"You don't have a key?"

"I lost it so I'll hit you when she get off unless you wanna wait til tomorrow?"

"Nah, just hit me when you ready."

"Gotcha."

"What was that all about?"

"I want to give him something to think about. I know he's gon' go back and get Jas."

"So we going to let him live?"

"Only for a minute."

"Frog I think we should off that nigga now, fuck waitin'!"

"Is that what you wanna do?"

"Yeah, why give him a chance to regroup." I called him back.

"Yo."

"What up?"

"We can handle it now. My folks just hit me."

"A'ight, I'll be there in 15 minutes."

"Damn Jas pick up ya phone."

After a few more tries I figured he probably had it on silent so I made my way over there.

"Hey, let me out so I can get in position."

"Remember, don't kill him in my shit."

"I got this, trust me."

"I always do."

Quick pulled up 10 minutes later. Instead of waiting on him I got out wit a bag and pistol in hand and walked to his vehicle.

"I would've came to you."

"It ain't bout nothing."

I passed tha bag of fake Coke. I started laughing when he started looking around.

"What's so funny?"

"You."

"Me?"

"Yeah you."

"Why am I so funny?" he asked still looking around.

"Who are you looking for, Jas?"

"Nah why would I be lookin' for Jas?"

"Let's see, for starters he's supposed to run down on me after you have tha work and only kill me if necessary."

"Where did you get that from?"

"That's what you said outta ya own mouth."

"I don't know who told you that but that's bullshit."

"Is it cause ya man didn't think so. He over in those bushes deceased."

He turned his head to look only to turn back around to have my .40 in his face.

"WHOOOOA WHOOOOA hold up Playboy there's been a mistake."

"I know, tha mistake being trying to rob me."

"I don't know what you talkin' bout, I swear."

"I don't believe you, if you weren't trying to rob me then where is my money for my shit?" He went to reach under his seat.

"Don't Fuckin' Move!"

"I was just trying to get tha money."

"Don't worry I'll get it, all I want you to do is sit back and relax."

Bones opened tha back door and slid in.

"Oh don't worry about me. I just came to count tha money."

"Under tha driver seat."

"Ain't no 75 large fitting under there," he said reaching under and coming up wit a big and a pistol.

"Damn, you was gonna try to shoot a brother, huh?"

"Nah, I was just going to get ya money."

"Bones how much is in there?"

"Hold on," he said acting like he was counting, "41 large."

"Nah, it should be 52 grand. You still 23 short."

"I was gonna hit you back wit 30."

"You should've told me that from tha gate."

Before I could say, anything else Bones put one in tha back of his head, causing it to slam against tha steering wheel.

"Now wipe down anything you touch and let's go."

"Let's put Jas is in tha car wit him and Burn it."

"Nah, let's just pour gasoline on 'em."

"I'll handle it just bring tha car."

"Hello."

"What tha biz Little Homey?"

"That problem was solved."

"So it was what you thought it was?"

"Yeah, but we were two steps ahead so we seen it coming."

"A'ight just checking up on yall, that's all."

"I appreciate that, I also need to get at you when you ready."

"You gotta give me about a hour; I'm not around right now."

"Just hit me up when you ready."

"I got you Little Homey." (Click)

"Is everything good wit them?"

"Yeah, they sent them New York cats to tha boneyard."

"Take a ride wit me on tha hill so I can drop this work off to Coop and Swish."

"Nigga you a'ight, them Dominican dudes ain't up there."

"Fuck you, I ain't worried about them!"

"You can't even take a joke."

"Not that kind anyway."

"Come on before I change my mind."

"If they came through here it would a lot of bloodshed."

"I know it's j-peed out here." I spotted Coop then hit horn to get his attention.

"You should've called to let me know you was in route; let me get that change for you."

"Take this wit you," I said, handing him tha bag wit tha work in it.

"Pull over."

"We might as well grab something to eat off tha grill."

"That's not a bad ideal."

"Hey Tiz."

"Hey."

"You still playing hard to get?"

"I was never playing hard to get."

"Well, you won't give me tha time of day."

"You been around tha block too many times for me."

"Boy please, Fire got you open like a window."

She must've noticed my facial expression because she said, "Yeah, I know about you and Fire; who does not? I've never seen you as tha one woman man type she must got that snapper."

"I wouldn't know nothing about all that."

"I know you ain't sprung like that and didn't even sample tha goods yet."

"There's my cousin right there."

"Let me find somewhere to park."

"Fire there go Tiz wit hot ass Sheeva all in his face."

I tried to play cool, but I knew what type of broad she was.

"Park right there," I said, pointin' to a spot where somebody was pulling out.

"It's packed out here."

"You know it's Hilltop Day."

"Oh yeah, I forgot."

"Hey Tiz, Fresh."

"What up yall?"

"I see you got ya groupies hanging around." (Ha! Ha! Ha!)

"Wow, I see you still didn't get over that little incident wit Frog."

"I always say a hoe is gonna be a hoe."

"A hoe that ya man just had to have."

"Ya best bet is to leave before a beat that ass again."

"Try it Bitch!" Val went to step up when Coop grabbed her arm.

"Don't stoop to her level. You better than that."

"Sheena, this is for tha kids and if you can't respect that then leave."

"Like I said Tiz you too sexy for that."

"And like I said, you been around tha block too many times for me."

"Fresh you need to school ya boy; how can he be siked for a broad that he never fucked?"

"Excuse me."

"No excuse me," Sheena said walking away.

"OOOOH I can't stand that whore ass bitch!"

"So what was that all about if I can ask?"

Of course, long story short, she was just saying how I was open wit out getting tha panties."

"How does she know that?"

"Because when she said you must have tha snapper, since I was open like a window."

"What does…"

"Let me finish," I said cutting her off.

"Finish."

"I told her I didn't know nothing about that and she went from there."

"Why didn't you just let her talk?"

"I don't know, maybe I just didn't want her to get some bullshit started like Rell almost did." At that moment I knew Tiz was someone I would be wit for years to come.

"Imma hit ya phone later."

"You don't have to leave because I came."

"I'm not I only came up here to holla at Coop."

"Damn Fire you still looking good as hell." I turned around to see who was talkin'.

"You need to stop frontin' and holla at a nigga wit some real paper."

"Aye Jr. don't disrespect me."

"Nigga who are you to be disrespecting?"

"You know what time it is, don't front."

"Nigga all I know is my money long and you can work for me if you need a job."

"Imma act like you just didn't say that dumb ass shit."

"When you get ya paper come up holla at me."

I was pissed. I really wanted to pull my pistol out and pop his dumb ass, but there were too many witnesses out.

I could see the way Des, Val, and Fire were all looking at me, so I said, "Jr. you can try to impress them but at tha end of the day you work for me."

"Oh yeah, imagine that you broke."

"Now you gonna make me pull your card, Trey ya boss."

"Who?"

"Trey, you know the one that fronts you work. Well, I front him work so that puts you on my payroll."

"Whatever Nigga."

"It is Wht it is, so next time you try to shine, you might wanna have ya facts right."

I could tell that not only was he pissed, but he was embarrassed.

"Like I said you broke, and when you want a job holla at me."

Fresh started laughing, he think it's a joke. Because it is. I looked at Des and Val because if nothing else, I learned that Tiz don't be lying or fronting.

"I can have you cut off just like that," he said snappin' his finger.

"You could never ever do no shit like that."

Tiz pulled out his phone, dialed a number then put it on speaker so we could hear.

"Yo, what up I was gonna hit ya phone."

"Listen Trey, you still fuck wit that nigga JR?"

"Yeah, why what's up?"

"Nah, he's talkin' all this money shit and how I can work for him."

"Are you serious?"

"Yeah, so as of this point on, cut him off; don't front him no more work just give him what his money pay for."

"Done deal."

"I got some big shit for you this go round."

"A'ight, hit me when you ready."

When he hung up Tiz said, "It is what it is!"

JR didn't say shit he just walked away. Now I didn't want to do that but he got above himself. He walked off like a scolded kid. I couldn't do what I really wanted to do, so he got tha next best thing embarrassed. I know if it was me, I would feel stupid talkin' shit to a mafucka who happened to be my bosses boss.

"Let me clear tha air. I'm not one of those dudes that brags or boast about all tha money I have or make, but when you get above yourself Imma put you in ya place."

"You don't have to tell us we already know."

"Cuz yall going to the Divas vs Don party tonight?"

"I don't know Swish was saying something about that earlier."

"That is tonight I forgot all about it."

"Come on Fresh I need to handle this other biz-ness."

"So, will I see you tonight?"

"You should."

"I hope so," Fire said, kissing me.

"He'll be there I promise you and I never make a promise I can't keep."

"Imma hold you to that Fresh."

"Come on we out."

"Damn, I wish he didn't have a girl."

"He is fine."

"Yes he is, but I would never mess wit anybody's man that's not my style."

"What if he tried to holla at you?"

"I still wouldn't holla at him."

"Mmm Hmm whatever bitch."

"Seriously if I had a man I wouldn't want nobody doing that shit to me."

"Me either."

"From tha looks of things you don't have to worry about that."

"I hope not because I don't think my heart could take that again."

"Then you'll be blaming us since we did tell you to give love another chance."

"I sure will."

"Well, I'm glad we won't have to worry about that."

"Sheena did make a good point."

"What point would that be?"

"Tiz really likes you and you haven't given him any punanny yet."

"Or has she?" Val asked.

"No I haven't, but when I do you two bitches will be the first to know."

"Des, she ain't had sex in so long that shit like virgin pussy." Ha! Ha! Ha!

"For your information anytime I get horny I always get my thing off."

"So do I but it's not like tha real thing, trust me."

It's been 5 months and Tiz still hasn't tried to have sex wit me. It made me think about what he said when we first started talkin'. *I know you think I just want to be that one nigga to say he finally knocked Fire off but ya wrong if and when it happens it'll be because you wanted it to."*

"What you smiling for?"

"I was just thinkin' about something Tiz said to me."

"Unh, Unh, Unh."

"What?"

"You just as open as he is and I think it's cute."

"I'm not open I'm just happy, that's all."

"WHAAAAT EEEEEVER."

"I would hate to see how you gonna act when yall finally do have sex."

"She gonna be like a little kid in a candy store."

"Cuz we bout to bounce, I'll see you at tha party tonight."

"No doubt first round on me."

"I'm a hold you to that."

"It's 6 o'clock drop me off so I can get me a power nap in."

"I feel you on that. I'm about to do the same shit."

CHAPTER 13

Tiz and Fire

"Flacco I think that it's time to come down and show you how to become a force to be reckoned wit."

"I think too much time has elapsed I'm ready to get back on tha grind."

"You still dealing wit that female?"

"Yeah, she's had my back through all this."

"A'ight, keep her we could probably use her to set these Niggaz up."

"She'll do what ever we need her to do."

"Good, I'll be down in a few hours."

"Hey."

"What's up Madi?"

"How much longer? I'm ready to send him to tha boneyard; I can't take no more."

"What's wrong?"

"He's always up my ass."

"It'll be over real soon."

"I think his Connect might be coming down in a few hours."

"How do you know that?"

"I overheard him on tha phone a little while ago."

"OK find out everything you can then get back wit me."

"Gotcha."

"A'ight, I gotta get dressed for this party tonight so find out all you can for me."

"You know I will Papi"

"I decided to get dressed at home instead of Iciss's."

I had just put my frames on when Killer, Tiz, and Fresh pulled up. (Beep,

Beep, Beep)

"I heard you Niggaz pull up. No need to go all crazy wit tha horn."

"My bag Playa. I see you got that Louis V on."

"I'm sorry but this Armani."

"Damn, Playa Playa you must of went shoppin' wit Iciss."

"I did, but I picked this out. I do have a sense in style."

"It was only a joke no need to catch feelings."

"I just want to have a good time tonight."

"You will, now light this up," Killer said handing me a blunt.

"Fresh you got one of those e-pills for me?"

"I thought you don't fuck wit them?"

"I don't, only on certain occasions tonight being one."

"I heard that. Here take this Blue Dolphin."

"Is this the one I had last time?"

"Yeah."

"Oh it's on tonight. Pass tha Bombay."

"Bombay? You mean Rosesay."

"What ever, I just need to take this e-pill."

When we pulled up at tha Chase Center it was packed. Tha line was around the corner.

"It's only 11:30 and tha line is this long." We all stepped out looking like a million bucks.

"Killer give me a shot of that Furdose; I know you've got it in tha glove box." We went to tha front of tha line to VIP.

"What up Heem?"

"I can't call it Big Rick."

"400 for VIP apiece?"

"No for all y'all."

"I got it," Tiz said pulling out his money.

"Pay inside."

"A'ight, when you get a chance come find me I'll buy you a drink."

"OK, I'll see you inside."

"Daaaamn look at yall; there's no doubt who tha real dons are."

"Yall know her?"

"No."

"Nah, Unh Unh."

"Me either."

"You can't blame her for recognizing tha sharpest Niggaz in tha party."

"I heard that, now let's hit tha bar; first round on Heem."

"It ain't bout nothing."

We went to VIP to get our drinks since tha other bars were crowded. Wow was all I could say when I was seen Iciss.

"Damn, I definitely know who tha diva is tonight."

"I bet you say that to all tha girls."

"No, just tha ones I love."

"Oh so you love me?"

"A little."

"Well, I need to get you to love me a lot."

"Nah you know I love you lots. I must say that dress looks damn good on you, I might have to hurt somebody tonight."

"No you won't. I only have eyes for you," she said kissing me.

"It's not you I'm worried about, it's them," I said pointing to tha guys staring at her.

"I already checked them."

"What are you drinking?"

"Same thing you drinking."

"Rosesay and Bombay."

"Well then, so am I."

"Come on yall we don't want to cramp their style."

"Turk speak for yaself; Iciss is wit me tonight."

"Excuse me."

"I told you once he seen her in that dress it was a wrap for her," Chaz said laughing.

"I don't know about yall, but I am going to get my party on."

"Wait for me."

"Lexis."

"What?"

"Don't forget you are pregnant."

"Boy shut up. I got this."

"Babe, go head I'm not going to hold you hostage."

"You not, I'm wit you tonight."

"That's all it is then, let's dance."

"What's up Fire?"

"Not you so beat it!"

"You still acting like ya shit gold."

"I told you that you will never get tha time of day."

"That's what ya mouth say but ya body is saying something totally different."

"Stan if you don't beat it, she got a man."

"He can't take care of her like I can."

"What ever."

"Believe that."

"You just won't quit."

"You can't have a man because if you did, he would never let you come out tonight wit that on."

"He would if he wasn't insecure," Tiz said walking up and putting his hands around my waist.

"Oh shit is this you?"

"Yeah this is my wifey."

"My fault I didn't mean no disrespect."

"None taken."

"I got that for you too I was going to hit you in tha a.m."

"A'ight just hit me up. Where are ya boys?"

"They around here somewhere. Next bottle on me."

"I'm good but thanks anyway.

Wow you really got a lot of money, power, and respect in this city."

"Des you gotta give respect to get it."

"Well, you must give a lot."

"What yall drinking lets hit tha bar."

"Before tha night is out you think I can get a picture wit you?"

"Fire you can get whatever you want."

"Why can't I meet somebody like you? I see ya boys came out wit their girls tonight."

"Yeah that's how they do."

"That's some real shit."

We had a ball except for a few Niggaz, who had to be checked.

"Tiz tell ya boys you riding home wit me."

"I need to get my car."

"I'll take you to ya car in tha morning."

"A'ight, I'll be right back."

"Yo, Imma ride wit Fire. I'll get wit yall tomorrow."

"Cool. Maybe you'll get lucky tonight." (Ha! Ha! Ha!)

"Fuck yall!"

"Nah Nigga you better try that shit on Fire." They all started laughing.

"Did I miss tha joke?"

"I think we both did, come on we out."

"Tiz."

"Yo."

"We love you man," they all said in unison.

"I love you Niggaz too. Yall more like brothers than boys."

I'll lay down my life for any one of them, and they would do tha same for me. Des dropped us off at my house.

"Hey Fire."

"Yeah."

"Don't be afraid to give a little," she said winking then pulled off. As I got in tha house, I poured me another drink.

"Do you have some wraps?"

"On top of tha fridge. Make yaself comfortable, I need to take a shower."

Well, she did that I rolled my weed and put on some music.

I FINALLY FOUND THA NERVE TO SAY I'M GONNA MAKE A CHANGE IN MY LIFE STARTING HERE TODAY. I SURRENDER ALL MY LOVE I NEVER THOUGHT I COULD. I'M GIVING ALL MY LOVE AWAY AND THERE'S ONLY ONE REASON THAT I WOULD AND BABY IS

YOU."

"What do you know about this?"

When I didn't answer she asked again.

"My bag, I was in a zone this my shit."

"I didn't know you like R&B."

"You'd be surprised; I'm not just a rap dude."

"I said when I found tha right guy I will get married off this song."

"Play ya cards right and I might be able to help you out wit that."

"Is that right?"

"It's ya choice. I am in it for tha long-haul."

I don't know if it was tha weed, a pill, or drinks I had in me, but I saw Tiz in another light.

"Would you mind if I jumped in tha shower? I don't like to go to sleep, sweaty."

"Sure tha towels are in tha closet next to tha bathroom."

"Do you have a dryer?"

"Yes why?"

"Imma wash my boxers out."

"What size do you wear?"

"34–36."

She walked in her bedroom and came back wit a brand new pair.

"You sure he won't mind you giving me these?"

"Don't be disrespecting me ain't no he but you. I wear these to bed sometimes."

"My fault. No need to get mad Baby Girl."

"I'm not none of those other broads you used to dealing wit if I'm wit you then I'm wit you, nobody else."

"I know that."

"It's been 5 months, you should."

"Let me jump in tha shower and then we can talk til we fall asleep."

Fire was so sexy in that nightgown. It was definitely going to be hard to be in tha same bed and not touch her. While he was in tha shower, I took tha liberty to pleasure myself because that E-pill had me so horny.

"You can put ya clothes on tha rack over there. Who told you to light my weed up?"

"What's yours is mine and vice versa."

"Are you sure about that?"

"Positive."

"Do you think I can smoke wit you?"

"Of course you can here," she said, passing me a blunt.

"What's this for?"

"Roll ya own."

"Wow."

"Hey."

"I rather smoke a wrap so Imma going to get one."

"Can you bring that bottle of Remy back wit you?"

"I guess."

When he got up I couldn't help but notice how big he was. Just tha size of it made me more horny.

"Babe, do you already have a couple cups?"

"No just one." I couldn't front that E-pill had me feeling good.

"Fire I need to be honest wit you."

"I knew you was too good to be true; how long you've been wit her?"

(Ha! Ha! Ha!)

"I really don't find this shit funny."

"I do because it was nothing to do wit no broads."

"Well, then what is it?"

"My boys were always telling me I need to settle down like them. And I told them if I could find a female like they had I would. Truth is, I never thought I would until 5 months ago. I knew you had me when I stopped dealing wit all my friends. Even if you don't believe me," I said, looking straight into her eyes, "for tha last 4 ½ months I haven't had sex."

"You said 4 ½, we been messing for 5."

"I know, tha first two weeks was a trial run."

I looked at him in his face and knew he was telling me tha truth. All I could do was pull him close and kiss him passionately. The next thing I knew I had my hand or his penis feeling it grow inside my hand. I wanted to stop, but my heart was telling me not to.

"Stop."

"What's wrong?"

"I don't want you to do this because tha weed and alcohol telling you to."

"It's not tha weed or alcohol is my heart."

Wit that said, I grabbed her in my arms and gently laid her down and begin to take her nightgown off.

"Tiz please be gentle, I haven't had sex in over 18 months."

"Trust me, it will be tha best sex you ever had."

Once I had her clothes off, I gently caressed her body wit my tongue and hands.

"OOOOOOH Baby that feels SOOOOO GOOD!"

I eased my way down until I got to her vagina. Then I massaged her clitoris wit my tongue which made her scream out in pleasure. I could tell she wanted me to put it in, but I was far from done wit the foreplay. When I turned her over on her stomach, she arched her ass up in tha air, just enough for me to put my tongue in tha crack of her ass.

"Oh shit, Oh Shit!" she screamed trying to get away. I pulled her back and continued to give her tha biz-ness.

"I-I-I-I can't believe this."

"What's wrong?" I asked but already knowing she was cumming."

"I'm Cumming!" I grabbed a hold of her clit and begin sucking it like a piece of candy.

"OOOOOOH SHIIIIIIIT I'm Cumming again! Oh My God Tiz please stop. I can't take no more!"

I turned her back over slowly, kissing her body. "Hold on she said getting up."

A few seconds later I heard, "NOW EVEN THOUGH I TRY TO PLAY IT OFF I'M THINKING ABOUT YOU ALL DAY LONG. I CAN'T WAIT FOR SHAWTY TO COME THROUGH FROM YOUR LIPS AND BACK UP TO YOUR EYES, MY HANDS ON YOUR HIPS WHEN WE GRIND FANTASIZING BOUT WHAT I'M GONNA DO TO YOU. GOT ME FIENING FOR HER LOVE CAN'T LIE MAN YOU SHOULD SEE HOW SHE GOT ME SPENDING ALL THIS TIME WIT HER AND I COULD LEAVE HER, IF I WANTED TO LOVE I WANTED TO. HER LOVE, TURNS MEN INTO FOOLS. TELL ME WHAT A MAN IS TO DO."

"Let me find out you can sing."

"I'm tha shit." I slid half my man inside her.

"OOOOW."

"I'm sorry, you want me to stop?"

"No, just take it slow."

I did just that slowly easing tha rest of my penis in. Once she was adapted to me, I gave her the biz-ness.

"CUZ I CAN'T BREATHE WHEN YOU TALK TO ME. I CAN'T BREATHE WHEN YOU'RE TOUCHING ME. I SUFFOCATE WHEN YOU'RE AWAY FOR ME SO MUCH LOVE YOU TAKE FROM I'M GOING OUTTA MY MIND."

"Yes Baby that's tha spot, I'm about to Cum." I took my finger and massage a clit which sent her over tha edge.

"YEEEEEES OOOOH YEEEEEES!" When I felt she was done I hit her spot again.

"I'm Cumming again Oh My God what are you doing to me!" After about another 6 nuts, she tapped out so I rolled offer her.

"Tiz I love you."

" I bet tha neighbors know my name."

"Shut up," she said punching my arm.

"So I guess this makes it official?"

"I thought we already were."

"Yeah, but this seals tha deal. I see why you haven't gave anybody any, as good as it is, you would have tha average Nigga going crazy."

"Yeah, well I see why all tha broads were talking about you."

"They didn't get it like you got it, that's for sure."

"I hear you."

"I'm serious." I ended up falling asleep while she went to wash up.

"Unh, Unh, Unh, look at him, sleep like a baby."

He wasn't lying when he said it would be tha best I ever had. I decided to get some rest because it was on again when we got up.

CHAPTER 14

Waitin' for tha Green Light

"Madi this is Nadal."

"Hello Papi."

"Flacco I see why you like her so much; she is beautiful."

"Thank you Papi."

"No need to thank me I'm just stating tha truth."

"Madi if you'll excuse me, we have important business to discuss."

"No problem, I need to go to tha supermarket to pick up a few things for dinner."

"Hello."

"Hey Madi."

"Hey, I finally got to see his Connect."

"What was his name?"

"Nadal."

"Where are you now?"

"On my way to tha market."

"OK when you get back I need you to take a picture wit ya phone and send it to me."

"No problem."

"Madi."

"Yes Papi."

"Be careful."

"I will, I just wish you would give me tha word so I can end tha charades."

"Soon mama soon."

"Asalamu Alaikum."

"Wailakum Salam."

"How are you doing?"

"Today is a good day for me Hum-du-Allāh."

"Well, I need some of your Hikmah (wisdom) and Naseehah (sincere advice).

"I'm always here to offer you that."

"Madi called she said that Flacco's Connect was down here. His name is Nadal. Does it ring a bell?"

"I heard that name somewhere before. I just can't remember where."

"She also said that she's ready to put tha baby to sleep."

"What do you think?"

"At first I didn't think we needed to but now since his Connects come down, they might be planning something. I don't wanna tell you to wait then it be too late. Give it a week if nothing happens tell Madi to disappear."

"And if something happens?"

"Give her tha word to send him to be wit his boys."

"Has Milan called you?"

"Nah, he must of picked up on tha vibe."

"How long has it been?"

"Two weeks."

"He's most likely on vacation he does that a lot."

"Did Sly come up wit anything on him?"

"No, he seems to still be on tha up and up."

"Heem, I will say this, if you feel in ya heart that Flacco is going to be trouble do what you need to do.”

“Thanks Asalamu Alaikum.”

“Wailakum Salam.”

“Papi I need your help wit these bags.”

“I thought you were only getting a few items for dinner?”

“I was but you know how that goes. Where is your peoples?”

“He left.”

“Will he be coming back?”

“No.”

“I bought enough for him to join us for dinner.”

“Madi, I may need you to do something for me in a few days.”

“What is that Papi?”

“I’ll let you know if I need you to do it.”

“OK you know I’ll do whatever you need me to do even if it’s to kill somebody.” She had no idea that was exactly what I might need her to do. I had a feeling that Heem was responsible for tha deaths of Juan, Dominic, and Jose.

“Flacco, Flacco.”

“Huh?”

“What were you thinking about just now?”

“My boys.”

“Oh I’m sorry.”

“No that’s cool.”

“Do you know my best friend was murdered a year ago.”

“I’m sorry to hear that.”

"They tried to kidnap her so they could get money from her uncle."

"He didn't pay?"

"Yeah, he pay but they still killed her."

"Where did they go?"

"To tha cemetery he found out who they were then killed them. I say that to say, I know it hurts. I think of her often." I made tears come to my eyes to make it more believable. He fell for the bait and put his arms around me to comfort me. I really poured it on then.

"Don't worry, I'll make sure you're a'ight, I promise."

"You better worry about yourself not me," I thought to myself wit a smile on my face.

"What would I do wit out you Papi?"

"Let's hope you never have to find out."

"You thought this was a game, didn't you?"

"I told you I would get tha rest of ya money."

"I gave you two weeks and its been three, so where is my money?"

"I have to go get it."

"Now see if I let you go get it you're going to run off and I won't see you again for a while Shit you'll probably leave tha state."

"I wouldn't do that Killer I swear on my life."

"You know, I think I should just end all tha games right here right now," I said, pulling out my Desert Eagle.

"Please No!"

"Do me a favor don't beg it will only upset me."

"I have your money."

"How come you didn't call me then?"

"Honestly, I was going to flip it then call."

"How bout we go get my money together that way it won't be no funny stuff going on."

"I'll have my cousin bring it here."

"Now do I look stupid to you? You know what, call ya cousin have him bring tha money but I promise you if he tries anything both of yall will die." I listened to his conversation to make sure he didn't try to throw no codes in.

"I can't believe you going through all this for 10 grand."

"First of all, it ain't about tha money and secondly, if it was, it's my money. You just need to be happy I'm gonna let you live."

30 minutes later, his cousin was knocking on tha door. I was surprised when a female came through tha door.

"Ain't you Tiz people?"

"Yeah."

"I'm Fire's best friend Des."

"What's up?"

"Not too much, here Stink you know aunt Karen had a million questions."

"I would've gotton it but I was tied up."

"Well, I gotta meet Fire and Val so I'll call you later."

"Stink I believe that you got it in you so Imma hit you wit some more work."

"Look Killer I know I messed up but Imma show you that I get at a dollar."

"A'ight we gon' see Imma hit you wit a half brick this time. Stink don't fuck my money up."

"I'm not."

"I hope you don't cause I like you."

"You'll see."

"Imma have somebody drop it off to you in tha next hour."

"Hey yall."

"Hey girl."

"Bitch you got some dick last night."

"What are you talkin' bout?"

"It's written all over ya face, now spill it."

"Giiiiiiiirl Wheeeeew he must be a plumber, tha way he lay pipe."

"Unh, Unh."

"He definitely knows how to put it down. I bust so many nuts I lost count."

"Bitch you lying."

"I swear, he knows how to work all 10 ½ inches something serious."

"10 ½ now I know you lying to us."

"Why would I lie and to yall at that?"

"So he's definitely a keeper then?"

"Hell yeah!"

"Bitch bout time," Val said, dapping Des.

"You know I had to take my cousin Stink this money and when I got there Tiz boy Killer was there."

"They really got tha city on smash."

"Yup, they definitely worth some money. Fire you got tha total package.

Too bad all his boys are taken cause I definitely would have told Tiz to hook a bitch up. Yall will never guess who I had breakfast wit this morning."

"Who?"

"Frog."

"How did that come about?"

"I went to Red's to eat, and he came in."

"And."

"And he asked me if he could join me."

"And of course you said yeah."

"Remember that night we was at tha Highway Inn?"

"Yeah."

"Tiz said that yall still liked each other but I told him you didn't."

"Girl, you know she still like or should I say love that Nigga."

"She should as long is they were together; he just made a mistake."

"Listen to you, why didn't you?"

"He cheated wit my cousin on more than one occasion so it was over, not to mention they are still together."

"His loss not yours."

"I say that's right."

"Fire I've never seen you wit such a glow not even when you were wit…"

"SSSSH you know tha rule on saying his name."

"Anyway, I'm just glad to see you happy."

"Happy ain't tha word."

"I need to find me a man like that."

"To top it all off he can sing his ass off."

"He serenaded you while sexing you."

"Yes."

"That would've made me cream all over myself alone. Fire you better hold on to him because guys like that don't come around too often."

"I'd be a fool to let him get away."

"I'll take him if you don't want him. Bitch don't be looking at me like that I'm just playing. She ready to snap over her man. I feel sorry for tha bitch to try to get him."

"So did you get lucky last night?"

"No comment."

"Awe shit this nigga finally hit tha skins."

"About time."

"No wonder he offered to treat us to lunch. That must've been one hell of a shot."

"Enough to make me hang my players suit up."

"Nigga you did that before you got tha ass."

"Hold up you're tha same Niggaz told me I need to settle down, wit one woman."

"We didn't think you would actually do it. And now that you have, I'm happy for you."

"Welcome to tha club."

"Tha club you said you would never be a part of." (Ha! Ha! Ha!)

"I did didn't I? Many have tried, but only one has succeeded."

"Cut tha bullshit."

"So on some more important things I'm about to give Madi tha green light on Flacco."

"You should've been done that."

"You ain't hear nothing from Milan?"

"No but Ahmad told me he probably went on vacation."

"We need to deal wit a few other problems, first being Rell."

"What's up wit him?"

"He tried to pay one of our peoples to put you in tha bone yard," I said looking at Killer.

"He's no problem, I'll handle him myself."

"Are you sure?"

"Matter fact, tell whoever he tried to pay to get back at him so we can set him up."

"Next up is Blake he's 30,000 in tha rear and talking shit."

"Every time I go through there he's never out."

"I heard he plays the Night Shift now."

"We've all been occupied as of late and a few people have taken advantage of it so we need to set the record straight."

"What do you want to do about those cats from River and South Bridge?"

"In tha next few days everybody will know that ain't nothing change."

CHAPTER 15

Tha Deal

"Yo, where can we meet to talk?"

"So you reconsidered my deal?"

"Yeah a nigga could use that cash."

"A'ight, meet me at Forman Mills in a half hour."

"Cool, I'll be in a blue Lumina."

20 minutes later, I was pulling up in tha parking lot. Rell pulled up wit some Shawty in tha car. He motioned for me to walk over to where my man was selling hotdogs.

"Let me have two beef, hotdogs, and one hot sausage wit onions and cheese."

"I'll take a beef sausage wit onions and cheese."

We stepped to the side so we could talk.

"So here's tha deal I'm going to pay you 3500 to hit killer up."

"Hold up, you said five stacks tha first time we talked."

"That was then this is now; either you want it or you don't."

"And all you want me to do is hit him up?"

"Yup I need him alive."

"I'll do it but I need tha money upfront."

"Nah, I'll give you 1500 now and tha rest when tha job is done."

"Make it 2500 and we in biz-ness." He went into his pocket and pulled out a wad of 100-dollar bills.

"How about you go wit me to make sure tha job gets done."

"That's a bad ideal," he said counting out 25 100-dollar bills.

"Be ready by 9 o'clock, I know where he'll be."

"Ok."

Ant had no ideal that after he did tha job he would be sent to tha bone yard. My motto no witness no suspects.

As soon as I pulled off, I hit Killer's phone.

"What's tha deal Ant?"

"Everything is set in motion."

"A'ight, bring him to 125 N. 35th St. just tell him I'm messing wit ya cousin."

"Gotcha."

"And you gotta make sure he comes in wit you."

"He will."

I met up wit Rell on Concord Avenue as we planned.

"Come on, my cousin just hit me. He's over her house so we'll catch him with his pants down, literally."

"I don't want to park on her block so we can park around here and slide in through the back."

"No problem, whatever works."

"Before we go in put this on," I said handing him a mask.

It was dark and quiet when we walked in.

"Where is ya gun?"

"I don't need one."

As soon as we got into tha front room tha lights came on.

"Don't you Mafucka's move!"

"What tha hell is going on?"

"You tell us, what tha hell yall doing in my house wit mask on? Matter fact, take 'em off right now!"

Ant took his off, but Rell didn't.

"I know you heard what he just said."

When Rell didn't move, I took my pistol and smacked him, upside his head.

"Pull tha Niggaz mask off Ant."

"Rell, did you really think I wouldn't find out what you were trying to pull off? Mafucka don't a dime get sold unless we know about it."

"Nigga fuck you!"

"Nah, fuck you!" (Pit, Pit, Pit)

"Help me wrap this Nigga up."

"Fuck!"

"What's up?"

"This Niggaz blood got on my Air Ones."

"You gotta burn them shits now."

Once tha body was wrapped up we put it in tha furnace in tha basement.

"Ant, you didn't see shit, did you?"

"See what?"

"Just making sure we are on tha same page."

"Come on man I would've pushed his shit back if you gave me tha green light; you know my work."

"I got a few jobs for you if you want to make tha money."

"Hey, you just said my favorite five letter word."

I put Ant down wit tha jobs and told him I would hit him when tha job was done.

"It's jumping out here tonight, Imma go grab some more work."

"They definitely coming strong tonight."

"Yo, what's up wit Heem and them?"

"Fuck them Niggaz!"

"That's all it is then."

"Next time they come through here they gon' to get something hot," he said, lifting his shirt and exposing his gun.

"I'm wit you."

"Niggaz claim to be making money but they sweatin' me for 30 grand."

"You got it."

"I know I do but them coming through made me say fuck 'em."

"Didn't you say ya cousin been coppin' from them for you?"

"Yup, I was gonna pay them get hit wit major work and burn 'em."

"Why didn't you?"

"Fuck 'em! How many you need?"

"I'm trying to spend 500 I don't want no dimes; I want a nice rock."

"Aye man come over here." I walked across tha street where Blake and his boy were at.

"How much did you say you had?"

"500."

"Where did a junky like you get 500 from?"

"Just because I get high doesn't mean I don't work. I'm part of tha reason you drive tha car you drive."

"Nigga you don't spend enough money to pay for my car."

"Are you sure about that?"

"Nigga look at you."

"Don't let this shit fool you."

"Mafucka fuck you and that 500 you got," Blake said, standing up.

"Hold on now no need to get hostile and go postal. I just want to spend my money."

"Give me ya money." I handed him my money.

"Now get tha fuck out of here!"

"What you want me to stand over there and wait."

"Nah Nigga you can step, you beat!" I turned my back and started walking.

"And don't bring ya ass back around here Fuckin' junky."

"Since you took my money, you might as well take this! (Boom, Boom, Boom, Boom, Boom, Boom, Boom, Boom)," I said, turning back around and letting off 8 shots hitting them both 4 times.

"Heem said take that 30 grand to hell wit you!" (boom)

"Hey whatever work and money you had of his just split it up."

"Good looking," they said as they hit tha stash spot then bounced."

I took my 500 back then jetted myself. I knew that if any witnesses saw tha only thing they could or would say was some junky shot them. I smile as I pulled out my phone.

"I still got it," I said to myself.

"Hello."

"Make sure you pick up tha paper in tha morning."

"I sure will. Are you coming to play ball tomorrow?"

"Nah Imma be at work but I'll play when I get off."

"A'ight, just hit my phone when you ready."

"No doubt I gotcha."

"That was Ant, Blake is in tha bone yard."

"Damn, he didn't waste no time. Do you think his boy will try to retaliate?"

"Nah, he offed him to just for GP."

"We gotta keep him on tha team."

"I'm about to hit tha crib before Lexis starts blowing my phone up."

"Damn Nigga you getting soft on me."

"Never that but wit her mood swings I try to stay on her good side, if you know what I mean."

"Unfortunately, I've never had to go through that, so no I don't."

"You'll see whenever you and Iciss decide to have kids."

"We got a long time for that. We don't want any kids no time soon."

"Better me than you, right?"

"You said it, not me."

"ALWAYS AND FOREVER EACH MOMENT WITH YOU."

"Hello. I'm on my way right now. OK I'll stop and get some. What I tell you and she wants me to pick her up ice cream."

"You got it bad, my brother."

"It ain't bout shit, that's my Baby."

"I heard that, I'll see you tomorrow."

My phone went off causing me to smile.

"Hey you."

"Hey, what time you coming in?"

"I was thinking about staying wit my young girl tonight."

"Oh you want to get her and you fucked up!"

"Nah, I'm on my way now. Did you cook?"

"Yes I did. That's why I wanted to know when you were coming in."

"How about I come in right now," I asked walking through tha door.

"Boy you gonna make me hurt you."

"Wow you already doing that wit them boy shorts on."

"Go wash ya hands so we can eat."

"I thought maybe we could go straight to dessert."

"Uh let me think about it, no, cause you know we won't even eat if we hit tha bedroom."

"I guess you're right."

"You guess? Boy you know I am."

"Like I said, I guess."

"Go wash ya hands."

"Yes ma'am. Iciss you think I can take a quick bath before we eat?"

"Yeah, you got a few minutes before tha potatoes are done."

Since I knew we would be getting it in I decided to pop a e-pill before I got in the shower.

"Heem, Heem."

"Yo."

"Just making sure you didn't drown in there."

"I'm drying off now smart ass."

When I came out Iciss was just sitting down to eat.

"Nice of you to join me."

"What's tha occasion?"

"Why does it have to be an occasion?"

"Because you cooked my favorite meal."

"I just figured since we haven't seen too much of each other all week. It was the least I could do to show you how much I missed you."

"We must've been on tha same page. That's why I got you this," I said pulling tha box out of my pocket."

"What is this?"

"Open it and see."

"A diamond heart necklace."

"Open tha heart."

"Oh My God, this is so beautiful Heem."

"Any time you start missing or thinking about me all you have to do is open ya heart."

"My heart is already open to you. I love you Heem."

"I love you more."

"Whatever."

"Baby this food is delicious."

"Thank you, I aim to please."

"You always do."

That night we made tha sweetest love that our bodies could dish out.

"So what so important that it could not wait til tha morning you had to drag me out of bed at 3:30 in tha morning."

"Listen, if it wasn't important I wouldn't even be sittin' here wit you."

"A'ight, I'm listening."

"I got a sting for you worth at least 6 figures but I need 100 grand."

"Now you got my full attention. I'm definitely listening now."

"You know Heem and his boys?"

"Yeah."

"I got tha drop on their main stash house."

"Is ya source reliable or what?"

"Of course or we wouldn't be even having this conversation right now."

"So how much is suppose to be in there?"

"At least a quarter mill."

"Then why not get it yaself?"

"Simple, you're a good at what you do. Besides, you hit one of their other houses."

"Nah, wrong dude."

"Slick cut tha bullshit, I saw you."

"How do I know this isn't a set up?"

"Because you're still alive."

"A'ight, so fill me in on all tha details and don't leave nothing out."

I told him a bunch of bogus stuff making it sound real.

"Take me back to my crib so I can get my tools."

"I've got a pistol if that's what you need."

"Where is it?"

"Look in tha back under ya seat."

As soon as he went to reach, I put a single bullet in tha back of his head, killing him instantly. I got out, wiped tha car down then left. I had one more stop to make before I headed home. I had about 45 minutes before tha sun came up, so I had to be in and out. I slid in through tha basement window, then made my way up to tha steps. I could see tha glow from tha TV in tha front room. There were two people asleep on tha couch. I screwed my silencer on and crept upstairs. I followed tha sounds of soft moaning to a bedroom in the back. When I walked in, I couldn't believe my eyes.

"I knew you couldn't be trusted, but my own cousin."

"I wish yall could see tha look on your faces."

"Baby, I can explain."

"Bitch don't say shit I came here to end ya life, but you are a bonus."

He tried to reach for his pistol (Pit, Pit, Pit) She started to scream out. I put my pistol to her mouth to shut her up.

"Baby I love you," she said, muffled.

"I loved you too." (Pit)

Her brains went all over tha headboard. I slid out just as quietly as I came in.

CHAPTER 16

Flacco Runnin' tha City?

"This is Lori Simms for tha Channel 2 News. There were 5 people murdered last night at 3 separate locations. As of now, tha police have no suspects or witnesses, we'll keep you up to date as tha stories develop. Lori Simms, Channel 2 News."

"Baby, did you hear that?"

"What?"

"5 people were killed last night."

"Damn they must of pissed somebody off."

"It was three separate incidents."

"Had to be something in tha water."

"Do you want to do some shoppin' today?"

"Sure, if you don't mind Chas going; we were going shoppin'."

"Yall go head, I don't want to intrude on girls day."

"You wouldn't be."

"Naw yall go ahead."

"You sure?"

"Yeah, I'll hang out wit tha fellas."

"Hey, did Gank call you about his young boy?"

"Yeah, that's a bullshit case."

"They found a gun in his house."

"Yeah, but he wasn't on probation so they had no right to even go in, let alone search."

"Wow, you are good."

"No correction, tha best."

"And you're cocky."

"Shouldn't I be as good as I am?"

"Yeah."

"Heem, I haven't lost a case yet."

"Tha other day in J-farmers and two guys come in talking about their case. One of tha dudes say man I ain't worried I got tha Jessie James of the court room Iciss Jones."

"Yeah, I heard that's what they call me. Who is Jesse James though?"

"He was a beast."

"Let me get going and I'll call you later."

"OK."

"If I see something you might like I'll pick it up."

"Do you need some money?"

"No."

"I knew you would say that."

"Why you ask then?"

"Baby it's a'ight to take my money."

"I know but why would I if I don't need it?"

"See you later."

"Heem."

"Yes."

"I love you."

"I love you more," I said back walking out tha door.

I stopped to pick up a newspaper, so I could see what went down last night. The only thing that was in there was tha Blake murder. "TWO MEN WERE MURDERED AND WHAT WAS TO BE BELIEVED IN A

ARGUMENT OVER DRUGS ACCORDING TO WITNESSES."

As I was about to make a call, my phone rang.

"Hello."

"Oh so you up?"

"It's 11:30. I'm not one of them all day sleepers. I should be asking you that you're tha one who had a long night."

"That was nothing but work for me. Where are you at so I can hit you wit ya money?"

"I'll get it. I know you good for it. Ant, how would you like a job on tha team?"

"I thought I already had a job on tha team?"

"You do."

"So there's no reason for you or anyone else to get ya hands dirty."

"Say know more."

"I gotta handle some biz-ness. I'll hit you up later."

"I'm around, you know how to reach me."

"I want you to meet my peoples because I have to leave town for a few weeks and I want you to hold it down til I come back."

"How come you didn't ask Mr. Rasato to run the biz-ness?"

Because you are my nephew and it's time you step up to tha plate because once I retire, you will have to take over."

"I'll be in Philly in 35 minutes."

"Flacco."

"Yes."

"Come alone."

"Milan, I would never bring anyone wit me."

"Not even that pretty Mamasha."

"No problem."

"Papi you OK?"

"Yeah, I need to take care of something, I'll be back in a few hours."

"Yo, this is Milan calling me now."

"See what he want."

"Yo."

"Hello my friend. How are you?"

"I'm good and you?"

"I just came back from tha Dominican Republic."

"Must be nice."

"I need to purchase 50 kilos."

"50?"

"Yes, as soon as I get everything in order I'll call you. Is that OK wit you?"

"Sure, just give me a call."

"What tha hell was that about? I thought we weren't dealing wit him anymore?"

"He spending 1.2 mil. That'll make anybody change their mind."

"We'll just keep, our eyes open for any funny stuff."

"Hey, I'm 10 minutes away."

"I'm at my house."

When I got there Milan was playing wit his daughter. Flacco!" she yelled running and jumping in my arms.

"Look at you getting all big. How old are you now?"

"6," she said, holding up 6 fingers.

"Come, Flacco let us talk."

Milan told me all that I would need to know about tha biz-ness on his end.

"We need to meet my peoples now. You ride wit Hector."

I was wondering why we were parked around here if I was to meet his Connect.

"What tha fuck are they doin' here?"

Oh shit I know that's not who he's been dealing wit all this time. I wanted to get out and say something but against my better judgment decided not to. Once we got back to tha house I asked Milan if that was his plug.

"Yeah why?"

"Those are tha guys I told you about."

"Heem and Killer?"

"Yeah and I think they had something to do wit tha murders."

"Are you sure?"

"I'm not sure if they murdered them but I'm sure that's them."

"Don't let them know that you know me; I got a surprise for them tha next time we meet."

"What do you plan on doing?"

"I'm going to stick them for 75 kilos'."

I couldn't believe my luck. My uncle didn't know it yet but that would be their last time alive.

"Do you have a backup plug?"

"Of course I do."

"I have to be honest if we don't kill them, they will retaliate."

"I have no plans on leaving them alive."

"Good, I just wanted to make sure we were on tha same page."

"Go back and lay low; will call them in a few weeks."

I knew deep down in my heart that this day would come, and once they're outta tha way, I will control Wilmington. It was after 9 o'clock when I got back home.

"Hey Papi, you're just in time for dinner."

"Smells good, what did you cook?"

"Steak, Spanish rice, and corn."

"Let me wash my hands first."

"Papi you seem like you're in a good mood."

"I'm in a wonderful mood. Things are about to get real good for us."

"How so?"

"I'll just say that in a few weeks I'll be running tha city."

"Oh Papi, you have more people coming down to help you?"

When he didn't answer I knew it was something else he had planned.

"Madi that was delicious."

"Thank you."

"I need a shower." As soon as I heard the water running, I called Heem to let him know what Flacco told me.

"He told you that?"

"Yeah but he wouldn't say anything more."

"A'ight, just keep ya eyes and ears open."

"Heem why don't you just let me kill him before it's too late."

"Too late for what Madi?"

"I don't know, I just have a bad feeling about this."

"Don't worry we'll handle it."

"A'ight, I gotta go. He's getting out of the shower."

"Madi be safe."

"I will, you do the same."

"Madi says Flacco is talking about runnin' tha city in tha next couple of weeks."

"How does he plan on doin' that?"

"He didn't say."

"Let's just put him to bed."

"He'll be sleep in tha next few weeks, I promise. Come on let's finish our work out."

"We finished."

"Nah, we still got to play that game of basketball."

"Are you sure you wanna lose?"

"Do you want to put some money on it? 100 dollars a game."

"100 nigga bet 200. It won't hurt you to lose a few hundred."

"If I lose."

"Game to 32 your ball," I said passing him tha ball.

(SMACK) "Where is tha fuck is my money?" (SMACK, SMACK) "Hold up Fresh."

"Nah Mafucka where is my money?"

"I-I-I-I got it."

"You got 30 seconds to get my doe."

"I need more time. I have to get it."

(SMACK) "Wrong answer."

"I need to get it."

"You got 15 minutes to have somebody bring my money."

"Can I make a call?"

"I don't care what you do but you have 15 correction, 14 minutes to have my money here." Crock made tha phone call and let them know he needed it and 10 minutes."

"Didn't sound like she was too happy."

"She'll be a'ight."

Five minutes later she was walking through tha door.

"Nigga next time you better get it yaself," she said throwing tha bag at Crock then storming out.

"You won't be getting none later. Do I have to count it?"

"It's all in there."

"Sure don't feel like 50 grand in here."

"Trust me, it is."

"You made me go through all that bullshit for my doe."

"I just got back in town a few hours ago."

"Well you should've let me know you were leaving town."

"It was a spare of tha moment thing."

"How was I supposed to know that? All I know is I call and you don't pick up for a few days."

"Fresh have I ever fucked up ya money before?"

"Nah but there's a first time for everything."

"I would've kept it 100 and let you know."

"Next time call a Nigga when you decide to leave on a spare of tha moment thing."

I put tha bag under my arm then made way out tha door.

"Fuck, you was bout to get left Nigga!"

"Yeah a'ight."

"For real."

"Hey Man, I had to get my change."

"Yo Shawty was bad as shit."

"Yeah and she was mad as hell for having to come over here."

"What he do flip it a few times?"

"Nah, he went away."

"I hope not wit Shawty cause if he did, she's ungrateful."

"Some broads don't appreciate shit. Drop me off at my crib."

"You going home?"

"Yeah, I gotta meet Turk so we can look at a few houses."

"Bout time yall buying a house."

"Not my ideal, hers if it was up to me, we would just stay in our apartment."

"Tha money you pay a month could be a mortgage on a crib."

"That's what Turk says."

"Hit me when you done."

Turk was coming out when we pulled up.

"Hey Tiz."

"Hey."

"I didn't think you was coming. I was about to leave."

"You said 12 o'clock."

"And it's 12:30."

"My bag, I had to handle something first."

"Yall have fun," Tiz said pulling off.

"Come on, we already running late thanks to you. We have to meet tha realtor at tha first house in 10 minutes."

"That's game."

"I had to let you win one or you wouldn't want to play anymore."

"Ha, Ha I heard that."

"Run it back."

"I'm done."

"Well you owe me 400; pay up."

"Damn Nigga Imma pay you."

"I gotta go take a shower and meet Iciss for lunch. I'll get wit you later."

"OK Imma shoot by tha ave and holler at Beefy."

"Hey there beautiful."

"Hey Baby, I'll be ready in two minutes."

"No rush, do what you have to do."

"Hey Chas."

"Hey Heem."

"You look like you're busy."

"Iciss has so many people trying to set up appointments. She's like some good weed everybody wants her."

"That's good for her; that means money, money, money, money and more money."

"Boy you crazy."

"I'm ready Iciss, don't forget you have a 3 o'clock."

"I know I'm only going to lunch."

Last time you two went to lunch you ended up taking tha rest of tha day off."

I looked at Heem, smiled, and said, "Hey, a bitch had to get her thing off."

"All I'm saying is you have appointments back-to-back this afternoon."

"I know and I'll be back in time. Do you want us to bring you back something?"

"No that's OK I ordered something from Minato's."

"Well see you when I get back then."

"Yup."

"Can we go to TGI Fridays? I really have a taste for that sizzling chicken and shrimp."

"We can go anywhere you want to go."

"Good, you're driving."

"We got an hour so let's get going."

"I'm glad it's not crowded in here."

"Two please."

The Waitress went to hand us a menu.

"We don't need it; we already know what we want."

"Oh OK."

"I'll have tha sizzling chicken and shrimp wit an ice tea."

"And I'll have tha Jack Daniels steak and shrimp wit water and tha boneless chicken tenders."

"A'ight I'll be back in a few minutes."

"Heem I've got this case where this guys baby mom planted drugs on him and called tha cops because he wanted to leave her alone."

"How do you know she put them on him?"

"Not only did he tell me, he has a recorded conversation of her admitting it."

"Is that admissible?"

"No but I've set up a meeting wit tha district attorney, so I'll see how that goes."

"I'm no lawyer but that'll probably be thrown out."

"I'm hoping so, because if not, it's going to be ugly trial." I was hungry as a homeless man.

"I see you didn't leave a trace of food on ya plate."

"That's because I didn't eat breakfast and I worked out and played ball."

"Did you win?"

"400."

"You got a gambling problem."

"No I don't."

"What do you call it then?"

"I'm just a person who likes to bet on things I know Imma win."

"Boy you funny, come on I gotta get back to work." I paid tha bill and left a 10-dollar tip which tha waitress appreciated.

"Don't get her hurt!"

"What are you talkin' bout?"

"You know what I'm talkin' bout. She's been smiling at you tha whole time."

"All I did was leave her a 10-dollar tip."

"You heard what I said."

"Iciss you know I only have eyes for you stop tha bullshit."

"Just making sure you still feel like that."

"Why wouldn't I?"

"I don't know."

"It took me too long to get you and I'm not giving you up."

"Will see you tonight?"

"Yes, just call me when you get off and I'll be over."

"That's another thing we need to buy a house instead of paying for two separate rents."

"Well, that means you plan on being wit me for a while."

"Unless you fuck up."

"That's not gonna happen."

"You better hope not. Don't forget I'm a lawyer, I know how to get away wit murder." We both started laughing.

"I love you," she said kissing me before getting out.

"Love you more," was my reply before pulling off.

"So you made it back this time?"

"We only had lunch."

"Judging by that big smile must've been one hell of a lunch."

"Get ya mind out of tha gutter; we went to TGI Fridays."

"I don't know, I thought maybe yall stopped for a quickie."

"Damn, why didn't I think about that. How long before my next appointment?"

"15 minutes, why?"

"I was going to call Heem for a quickie."

"Girl you crazy. I don't want to hear that."

"Well too bad," I said pulling out my phone."

"Saved by your 2 o'clock."

"He's early."

"I hope you don't mind but I have to take my girl to tha doctors."

"No, it's fine Iciss isn't busy."

I just look at Chas wit that Imma get you face.

"Follow me please. Now what can I do for you?"

"You represented my cousin Damon . Damon Brawny?"

"Yeah, he referred me."

"A'ight."

"Well, I was arrested for some bullshit."

"What are your charges?"

"First-degree assault, possession of a firearm and reckless endangerment."

"Did you have a gun?"

"No." After talking to him I knew I could beat this so I told him I needed 2,500 which he paid right there.

"I'll see you in court if you need me before then just call."

I handled tha rest of my appointments then went over my case for tomorrow.

"Hey, do you want to go to happy hour for a few drinks?"

"Sure, I could use a drink or two."

CHAPTER 17

Tha Crap Game

"How tha fuck did you let them run down on you like that?"

"They came through tha back alley."

"How much did they get?"

"5 grand."

"That's all?"

"Yeah."

"Do you have any ideal who it was?"

"I think it was that nigga Run from Riverside."

"How do you know that?"

"He has that tattoo on his hand that says pure shooter."

"Don't worry about it we'll take care of it."

"Frog we need to get at that Nigga ASAP. He know that's our work."

"I know that means he's saying he don't give a fuck and fuck us."

"Come on let's swing through there."

When we got over there, Run was in tha middle of a big dice game.

"What yall shootin'?"

"Hitting C-Lo."

Run looked up, "Yall want in?"

"Yeah, I got 50."

"I got 50 too."

"Trips, 4–5–6 is double pushers pay; oh yeah, 1–2–3 is double too."

"You gon, talk or roll tha dice?" somebody asked. He rolled trip 3's.

"Yall see it makes it look like something." His next roll was a 4.

"Bet something 4 or better."

"Bet 50."

"It's a bet." Bones rolled tha dice 1-2-3.

"Make it look like a hundred nigga."

"You want to bet 50, 4 or better too?"

"Nah, bet a buck."

"Bet it then."

Frog rolled tha dice tha first to die showed a 5 and 4 tha last rolled a 3. He picked up tha dice, blew on them, then let them go this time hitting C-10 4-5-6.

"Make it look like 200 and I got bank."

"Not if somebody else rolls C-Lo."

When everybody was done Frog had tha dice.

"How much is in tha bank?"

"Unlimited."

Since I knew Frog could shoot, I decided to bet wit him on 4 or better and give everybody else lays on 5 or better. Frog rolled C-10 tha first 4 rolls.

"Man, this nigga lucky as hell."

"Nah, it's skill youngin'."

Next time he rolled 1-2-3.

"Gotta pay my taxes I ain't mad at all."

"We ain't mad either; just make it look like something," said Run.

After about another half hour, nobody wanted to side bet wit me.

"Fuck this. Shoot some craps."

"I don't think yall wanna do that," I said knowing we were really going to clean them out.

"Put up or shut up!"

"That's right, talk that shit."

"They won't be talkin' after we take their money."

"Let me school these things," I said before rolling a door blow.

"This is gonna be like taking candy from a baby."

"Fuck this, bet a buck on tha come out."

I took all bets and let Bones get his bets before rolling. Little Joe bet a buck. Everybody tried to jump on my 4.

"I'm taking all lays."

"No problem, bet 10 or 4 too."

I rolled tha dice, tha first one stopped on 5 while tha other one spinned.

"You better catch that because it's a 5."

"Why would I catch a deuce?"

When it stopped spinning it was at 5.

"Bet back."

"It's a bet."

I hit three more 10s, then two 11s before finally hitting my point.

"Bones you wanna roll and get some of this easy free money?"

"Nah, you gonna shoot, you got my money."

"So do I," Bones said holding up his big knot.

"Fuck it, I'll keep shooting til I take it all."

A few Niggaz started betting wit me.

"What type of time you on now you going against tha grain."

"Fuck you Run. I ain't no fool this nigga hot I need to win my bread back."

"Bet wit me and you will."

I could tell Run was damn near broke, because he started betting less.

"Damn nigga you running outta money?"

"Ya shot."

"Nah you can go back."

"I'm done."

"You just gonna quit like that?"

"I really didn't come over here for this."

"You not gonna just win my money in leave!"

"Why not it's my money anyway."

"Fuck you talkin' bout Nigga?"

"My young boys you hit for tha 5 stacks earlier."

"What?"

"Stop playing games Run," Frog said pulling his .45 out, "let me see ya hands."

"Run held his hands out."

"Nah nigga turn 'em over." Sure enough he had Pure Shooter on his hands.

"Listen, I've got a proposition for you, give me tha money you took and you get to live."

"I don't know what you're talkin' bout." (Boom Boom) Bones hit him in his chest point blank range.

"Oh Shit!" Somebody yelled.

"Ain't nobody see nothing," I said dropping a wad of doe on the ground then stepping off.

"I told that nigga that stick up shit will get him put in a box," We heard somebody say while we were walking off.

"Next time, let me body a mafucka, will you."

"Hey man, you always wana do all that damn talkin'."

"Shit."

"What's up?"

"I missed Tiz call while we were shooting dice."

"Call him back."

"I'm bout to do that right now."

"Yo, what up Youngin'?"

"My fault, I missed ya call, but I was knee-deep in a crap game."

"That's cool, where are you at now?"

"On my way to tha block."

"I'll meet you at ya spot in 20 minutes."

"Aye, yo them Niggaz got tha Eastside in a serious chokehold."

"No thanks to me."

"Do you want me to ride wit you?"

"If you don't mind."

We drop tha work off, then headed to tha stash house for our weekly meet.

"Your Honor my client was illegally detained. They lied when they told him they had a search warrant, therefore making tha drugs non-permissible."

"Ms. Jones your client should have asked to see tha warrant."

"He did Your Honor which they showed him."

"Then what's tha problem Ms. Jones?"

"This Your Honor," Iciss said, pulling out tha warrant to show tha judge.

"Bailiff, could you bring that up here please?"

After a few minutes, tha judge said, "Ms. Jones I have to agree wit you to somebody who doesn't know this would appear to be legit, but as a person who knows tha law, I have no choice but to dismiss all charges."

"Thank you, Your Honor."

"Mr. Smith I want to say let this be a lesson to you. Next time you may not be as lucky, case dismissed."

"Thank you Ms. Jones."

"Hey this is what I get paid to do."

I was feeling a little horny and my schedule was clear for tha rest of tha day. I decided to call Heem to see if he could unclog my pipes. He picked up after tha third ring.

"Hey you."

"Hey Baby, are you busy?"

"Just finished up wit my meeting."

"Do you think you can come help a sista out?"

"What you need me to do?"

"I heard you tha best plumber so I need you to come lay some pipe!"

"You know I was gonna call you and see if you had some free time on ya hands."

"I have tha rest of my day free."

"Say no more, I'll meet you at tha house in 15 minutes."

"I'll be butt naked waiting."

"Hello law office of Iciss Jones."

"Chas it's me."

"What's up?"

"I'm taking tha rest of tha day off so if you want to do tha same, you can."

"Thank you boss."

"What I tell you about calling me that."

"Yeah, Yeah, Yeah I'll see you tomorrow."

On my way home Heem called to say he had to make a run and would be by in 45 minutes which was good because it would give me time to shower and get this Kitty Cat ready to be ate. When I got out of tha shower I dried off, lotion up, and laid across tha bed.

"Mmm that feels Soooo good." I thought I was dreaming until I open my eyes.

"I figured this would wake you up."

"How long you been here?"

"Long enough to take a bath now lay back down so I can finish my lunch."

2 ½ hours later, we were cuddled in each others arms discussing where we should take a vacation in tha next few weeks.

"I always wanted to go to Paris."

"How about Punta Canta?"

"Punta what?"

"Canta is in tha Dominican Republic."

"I don't know."

"I had a biz-ness trip coming up, so I figured why not knock out two birds wit one stone."

"Ahmad and Jada said it's real nice."

"Damn, you already had this planned, huh?"

"Something like that."

"Well, let me look at my schedule for tha rest of tha month and I'll let you know."

"A'ight but don't take too long. I wanna make reservations as soon as possible."

"I'll let you know no later than tomorrow, I promise."

"I need to handle some biz-ness, so I'll see you tonight."

"I gotta go by my mom's house anyway."

"See you later."

"Love you."

"Love you more."

"Boy please."

"Call me if ya mom cooked."

"You know she did."

"If you're not cooking, bring me a plate home."

"I was gonna cook but you got a sista worn out."

"Well just call me when you're on ya way back home."

"Will do. Oh yeah, before I forget tha Realtor called she said she found tha perfect house for us and wants to meet us at 12 o'clock tomorrow."

"A'ight," I said pulling out my iPhone to store that time in so I don't forget.

"LIFE'S A BITCH THEN YOU DIE THAT'S WHY WE GET HIGH. YA NEVER KNOW WHEN YA GONNA GO."

"Yo, what up Killer?"

"I need to holla at you. Where you at?"

"Leaving tha crib, meet me at tha park."

"I'm already here." Tha park was packed as usual when I pulled up.

"Heem what's tha deal playboy?"

"I can't call it Zack, what's good wit you?"

"Trying to eat, that's all."

"I heard that player."

"Heem can I have a dollar?"

"What I tell you about asking for money wit out speaking first."

"Hey Heem, can I have some money?"

"You are a funny dude. Here take this, go to Sports Connection, get you some sneaks and keep tha change," I said handing him a hundred-dollar bill."

"Thanks Heem."

"You know them was his play sneaks."

"I don't care. He needs to have a fresh pair then."

"Yo, you know that nigga Biz?"

"The one that be on Jefferson?"

"Yeah that one."

"What about him?"

"He's been askin' questions about you."

"What kind of questions?"

"I don't know, Cassy didn't say."

"Well, let's go find out."

"You got ya strap."

"Like American Express I don't leave home wit out it."

"Better to be caught wit it then wit out it," we both said in unison.

"Yo, where are yall on yall way to?"

"Up Jefferson to holla at Biz."

"Hold up, I'm coming."

"Tiz where did you cop those new Jordans at, they hot?"

"These ain't even hit tha stores yet. I gotta Connect."

"I need a pair of those."

"I got you."

"Hey Biz, let me holla at you for second."

"Hold up, let me take care of something real quick," he said dipping into his house.

"He went to get his heat."

"Why what's going on?"

"He's been inquiring about Heem."

"What's up yall?"

"I heard you had something you wanted to know about me."

"Who ever you got your information from told you wrong."

"Nah, I doubt it."

"Look Heem if there is something you want to say, just say it!"

"All I have to say is keep my name out of ya mouth or else."

"Or else what?"

"We gonna have a serious problem."

"I don't take kindly to threats," Biz said, pulling out his .38. I was about to pull out, but I caught something out of tha side of my eye that made me stop.

"Ain't no need for all that. I just came to talk because if I didn't you'd be dead already."

"Keep talkin' and you'll be tha one…"

Boom! Fresh popped him right in his top before he could get tha last word out.

"I think tha word he wanted to say was dead," Fresh said wit a big smile on his face.

"Come on, let's get out of here before tha cops come."

We put our guns up, then went back to tha park.

"How did you know we were up there?"

"I didn't, I was collecting some money from one of my young boys and I just happen to see Biz pull his pistol out."

"If I hadn't seen you tell me to fall back, he would have gotton more than one bullet."

"Do you think anybody will talk to tha police?"

"If we thought that you wouldn't be sittin' here right now."

"True."

POP, POP, POP, BOOM, BOOM, BOOM!

We all looked across tha park to see tha young boys from 7th shootin' at tha young boy from 6th and Blood Money. Wit in seconds tha police were everywhere. They gave chase to one of tha boys that was doing tha shooting.

"I'm getting tha fuck out of here it's hot as a firecracker."

"I hope tha young boy got away."

"If not, he better have bail money."

"Me and Fresh about to shoot a top yall wanna roll?"

"What yall going up top for?" "Do a little shoppin'."

"Nah, I'm good."

"Imma roll wit yall."

"We'll holla at you later Heem."

I decided to call Ahmad to check up on him.

"Asalamu Alaikum."

"Wailakum Salam."

"How you?"

"Tayib (good).

"Hum-Du-Allāh."

"What's been going on wit you?"

"Just trying to get this other shop together."

"Respect. Did you say something to Iciss about Punta Canta?"

"I did and she has her heart set on Paris."

"Just tell her you go to Paris when you get back because even if she doesn't go, you still have to."

"I know but I'm sure she'll go."

"Did Sly get back wit you on anything about Milan yet?"

"Only what I already told you."

"He hasn't hit me back, but I figured he'll be a little longer since he copped more this go round."

"Me and Jade are having a cookout this weekend."

"You know I'm there what you need me to bring?"

"Iciss."

"Imma make some seafood salad."

"That'll work."

"Where is AJ?"

"You know he's in tha game room."

"I don't even know why I ask. Well, I'll see you Saturday."

"A'ight make sure you tell tha fellas so they can come."

"I got you, don't worry about it Asalamu Alaikum."

"Wailakum Salaam."

I always felt refresh after talkin' Ahmad he's like my mentor slash big brother.

CHAPTER 18

Heem is Shot

"Listen, this is tha plan Imma gonna have him meet me, take tha work, then put him down like an old dog."

"Do you think he's going to come alone?"

"It doesn't matter if he does or doesn't. This will be his last sale he'll ever make."

"I take it you got everything set up wit tha new plug?"

"Yeah, everything is a go."

"A'ight, I'll talk to you Saturday."

"That's tomorrow."

"I know."

"You said it like it's days away."

"Let me rephrase it then, I'll see you tomorrow."

That night as I lay in bed, I couldn't help but smile as I thought about what was coming tha next day. In my heart, I knew I would be getting some payback for my boy. That night I finally got a good night's sleep.

"Hey, which one of these do you think I should wear today?"

"Neither, I think you should go wit tha peach dress."

"What peach dress?"

"Under tha bed in that box."

"Tiz I know you didn't buy me a new dress?"

"Yup, Donna Karen and a pair of open-toed shoes to show of those pretty feet of yours."

"What I tell you about buying me stuff?"

"Fire and what I tell you about that independent shit?"

"We gonna always bump heads so let's just agree to disagree."

"Don't we always?"

"I just seen this when I was up top and I knew it would look good on you so I bought it."

"Don't get me wrong, I love it."

"My boys they always buy their girls things whether it be clothes, roses or just a stuffed animal."

"Awe that's so sweet."

"That's why I do it, not that I'm trying to take you out of your independency I'm just showing you how much I care, that's all."

"How bout we call a truce?"

"Fine wit me."

"I might need this in writing."

"No you don't."

"What time does tha Bar-B-Q start?"

"I think 10 o'clock."

"I wanted to whip up some deviled eggs; we can't go empty-handed."

"We not I bought beer."

"I thought you said they were Muslim?"

"They are."

"You can't take beer."

"They Muslim we not."

"Boy you ignorant."

"No I'm not. We do this all tha time."

"Well, Imma whip these deviled eggs up real quick."

"Hey, do you I'm bout to blow me some weed."

"Heem you ready? I promised Jade I would help her out."

"So, you gonna walk around like that all day?"

"Boy no, I'm taking my clothes so I can change when I'm done."

"OK."

"And if I was?"

"You'd still look good to me."

"Good answer."

"I'm ready."

"Don't forget tha seafood salad."

"I'm not."

When we got there, Mom Sady, Ms. Taylor, and Chas were already there.

"You right on time to help me wit tha grill."

"Man, I'm not messing wit no grill today."

"You can always change ya clothes."

"I'm not Fuckin' wit no grill, point blank."

"Daddy I'll help you."

"Don't worry I got you," Maze said walking out onto tha deck."

"You're early."

"I figured you would need some help on tha grill."

"See you don't need me, Maze got you covered."

"You lucky."

"I did make some jumpin' seafood salad."

"Oh you definitely get a pass now."

"Well, I'll be in tha game room playing a little Madden."

"Tiz said he's bringing his girl."

"Yeah."

"Hold on, Tiz got a girl?"

"Yeah, he's been wit her for a while now."

"Is she pretty?"

"Maze she a Dime."

"That nigga finally settled down. I can't wait to meet tha broad that locked him down."

"Heem, are you helping them wit tha grill?"

"No!" Maze and Ahmad both yelled.

"Well, we need to run to tha supermarket for us."

"Ha Ha that's what you get."

"Yup, see you in about an hour."

"If he's lucky."

When I got in tha house they had a whole list they wanted me to get. I looked at Iciss, who just shrugged her shoulders.

"Do you want me to go wit you?"

"No, he's a big boy, besides you have to make tha crab cakes."

"Sorry Baby I tried."

I didn't say nothing. I just walked out.

"I am out for presidents to represent me."

"Hello."

"Hey Heem, my friend, can we meet?"

"Yeah, but I need about an hour. I'm in tha middle of something."

"OK just call when you ready. I need 75 this time. Can you handle it?"

"Milan, there isn't an order you can place that I can't handle."

"That's good my friend, real good."

After hanging up I made tha call I needed to make to have everything in place then I went to tha supermarket.

"Damn we were about to put an APB out on you."

"Yall damn near sent me grocery shopping all tha stuff on this list."

"Did you get everything?"

"Yeah but tha celery seeds."

"Thank you Baby," Ms. Taylor said.

"No problem, Iciss I need to handle something. I'll be back in an hour."

"I thought you said you was chilling today?"

"I was, but I just got a call that I need to take care of."

"Heem."

"Yes."

"I love you," she said, hugging me as if it would be her last time seeing me.

"I love you more but I'll be back."

"I know, just be safe."

I decided to make tha run by myself this time since it would be fast. For some strange reason I decided to have Craig stay in tha car wit tha work. Milan pulled up then got into my car. He put tha bag in tha backseat, then reached for tha room key that was in tha middle console.

"Hey my friend, I believe you met know my nephew," he said signaling for somebody in his car.

I couldn't believe my eyes when Flacco got out tha passenger side.

"Flacco's ya nephew?"

"Yes and I believe he has something he wants to say."

I went to reach for my gun but forgot I didn't have one on me.

"I wouldn't advise you to do that," Milan said wit his .40 in my face.

What is this all about? I believe you know the answer to that Flaco said now standing at my window. If I knew I wouldn't be asking. Dominick's, Jose, and Juan. Do those names ring any bells? No can't say they do. Those are my boys and you killed them. I could see the murder in his eyes and I knew I would leave in a body bag so I said I didn't kill them myself but I wish I had then spit in his face.

POP, POP, POP, POP, POP, BOOM, BOOM, BOOM, BOOM, BONG, BONG, BONG!

"AAAAH Shit! I'm hit let's get outta here."

Craig went over to me. I could hear him yelling for someone to call an ambulance. You have to get out of here before the cops come. I'm not leaving you. I see him run off then come back. I knew I was dying. I could see that white light. They always talk about so I make sure my last words will get me into junnah (paradise) La Ilaha Ill-Allāh (nothing has the right to be worshiped, but Allāh) then I said to Isis, I'll always love her La Ilaha Ill-Allāh and everything went black.

"Ahmad has Heem called you?"

"No."

"He's been gone all day and he's not answering his phone. Killer, Tiz, Fresh have any of you talk to Heem?"

"Nah I've been hittin' his phone all day."

"Me too."

"Iciss did he say where he was going?"

"No he just said he had to handle some biz-ness."

"I'm sure he's OK," Jade said.

Just then Iciss's phone rang.

"Boy were you at? Got me all worried."

"Iciss this is Craig, Heem has been shot. He's at Temple Hospital in critical condition. They say he's not going to make it."

"NOOOOO, NOOOOO!" she screamed dropping tha phone causing everybody to run outside.

"NOOOOO my Baby NOOOOO!"

Ahmad pick tha phone up said few words then hung up.

"Ahmad what's going on?" Killer ask wit a look of concern on his face.

"We need to get to Temple. Heem's been shot? He may not make it."

We all loaded up and hit tha highway. As soon as we got into tha hospital I spotted Craig wit his head down and Heem's blood all over him. Tha doctor was coming out at tha same time as this old white detective was walking up to Craig.

"I'm Detective Folly could you tell me what happen?"

"Listen detective like I told tha other three cops I went inside to get a room I heard gunshots when I got outside two men were runnin' from tha car."

"If you live in Delaware why were you gettin' a room in Philly?"

"We were surprising our friend wit a bachelor party."

"Did you see tha guys."

"All I know is they were Hispanic." As soon as he said that, I knew it was Milan.

"Here's my card. If you can remember anything else don't hesitate to give me a call."

"I told you everything I know," Craig said handing tha card back.

"I see why Heem liked this kid."

Once tha detective was gone tha doctor came back. He was looking around.

"I am his fiancé."

"Well, I'm sorry to say."

"Oh God NOOOOO please don't say it please NOOOOO." Mom Sady grabbed Iciss to comfort her.

"He's in a coma and I have to be honest he's probably not gonna come out. He was shot nine times close range."

"Can I see him?"

"Yes but you may want to consider taking him off life support."

"No! My Baby is coming back to me and don't you ever suggest that again!"

"I'm sorry, but I had to let you know, and this could be very expensive."

"Money ain't shit, I have plenty of it."

"And so do we," Killer said wit tha look of death and his eyes, "now take me to my baby's room!"

I almost lost it myself when I seen tha man who was like a little brother to me laying there wit tubes in his body.

"He's OK yall he's just catching up on his rest," Iciss said, trying more to convince herself than us.

"Maze, Killer, Fresh, Tiz, and Craig let me holla at yall out here for a sec. Craig do you know who it was?"

"Milan."

"You sure?"

"Positive I always come wit Heem to hit him."

"How much work did he get?" Killer asked.

"None."

"Huh?"

"Heem told me to get tha room but not put tha work in it."

"So where is tha work now?"

"When I saw what was going down I got out of tha car busting my .45, I hit one of them. He told me to leave but I wasn't leaving him there alone so I ran back to my whip, gave my pistol to my girl, and told her to go home."

"I respect that Craig I really do."

"How much work was it?"

"75 birds."

"You sure?" Fresh ask.

"Yeah, I would never take anything from Heem I love him like a big brother."

"Milan just woke up tha sleeping giant."

"Ahmad I think it would be best to move Heem to Christiana just in case Milan wants to finish him off."

"I'm already on it."

"Ahmad you know I can't let you do this wit out me."

"I figured you would not."

"Oh shit, tha legends are coming out of retirement. Do you guys still meet at tha house on Greenhill?"

"Yup."

"We'll meet there at 8 o'clock."

"Ahmad."

"What's up Craig?"

"I have nothing but respect for you, but I'm in on this no matter what yall say."

"I wouldn't have it any other way. You've already showed and proved ya loyalty."

"Ahmad I told you we should have left Sly on him."

"You did, but I didn't think it was necessary and I was wrong, now I'm paying for it."

Everybody came out tha room except Iciss. When I walked in, she was sitting next to his bed talkin' to him.

"Hey Sis, I'm having him transferred to Christiana Hosptial tonight, so we can't be closer to him and not have to worry about Milan trying to finish tha job."

"So you know who did this to him?"

"Yes I do."

"Is Killer and them going to handle it?"

"Yeah, along wit me, Maze and Sly."

"Ahmad I don't want you to do that."

"I feel I'm to blame for this, so no matter what anybody says I will not stand down."

"Baby."

"Yes Jade."

"Tha doctor said that Heem is about to be transferred to Christiana."

"That was fast, we better get going."

"I'm riding wit him. Yall can pick me up from there."

On tha ride back, I drove to let Ahmad clear his head. I could tell his heart was heavy.

"Baby I've never seen Iciss in so much pain."

"They don't deserve this."

"Do you know who did this?"

When he didn't answer, I looked over to see tears rolling down his face. I touched his hand, bringing him outta his daze.

"I'm sorry what did you say?"

From tha look in his eyes, I knew in my heart he was back in.

"Be careful I don't want to lose you."

"You won't, but I have to do this."

"I know just be careful please, me and tha kids need you."

"Kids?" he ask looking over at me.

"Yes, I found out yesterday when I went to tha doctors."

"How far along are you?"

"Only 6 weeks."

"I need you to drop me off at tha house. I'll be by tha hospital later."

Once I got in tha house I made Dua for Heem then made a phone call.

"Ahmad my friend, what is good?"

"Listen cut tha friend bullshit. I know it was you who killed my brother."

"I do no such thing."

"Now you insult my intelligence you Fuckin' Spic!"

"Is this how you talk to an old friend?" Milan ask smiling on tha other end of tha phone.

"Enjoy life while you can because I'm going to crush everything you love and when I'm done, Imma kill you!"

"My friend, you don't want to start a war, you surely cannot win."

"We'll see."

I hung up before he could say anything else. I called everybody and told them to meet me at the house right now.

Listen, you already know Milan is responsible for what happened to Heem. I talked to him a little while ago and he seems to think we can't win. What he doesn't know is I have goons in Philly that wanted to take him down for years but I outta loyalty and respect I had for him I never let them but now I take tha leash off tha dogs."

"So what do we do?"

"Once I talk to them I'll let yall know what time we'll be heading out."

"Hello."

"What's tha deal Tank?"

"Oh shit, what up Ahmad?"

"I got a situation I need to holla at you about."

"If I can be of some help, you know I will."

"Have you seen Milan?"

"Nah, I haven't seen him in months plus you're tha only reason he's still walkin' this earth."

"Well, he's no longer a friend of mine; I need to know where all his people live and all his blocks he run."

"Is everything cool?"

"Nah, that mafucka put my little brother in a coma."

"How tha fuck?"

"As you know, I was retired so I handed tha reins over to him. Milan called me a few months ago wanting me to point him in tha right direction."

"So you plugged him in wit ya brother?"

"Yeah, he tried to hit him for 75 birds but got nothing."

"I'll be happy to track him down for you."

"Me and a few guys want to assist you."

"No problem, when you coming up?"

"In tha next few hours."

"A'ight come to tha spot on Erie Ave."

"I'll hit you when we get close."

"Cool, no need to bring weapons we have plenty to choose from."

"There will be 7 of us."

"No problem, I'll be waiting."

I called everybody so we could meet up.

"Baby, please come back to me. I don't want to live my life wit out you."

I felt so helpless laying there not being able to respond but hearing everything. Madi walked in, I could tell she had been crying because her eyes were red and swollen.

"Oh, Heem, who did this to you?"

"That Fuckin' Flacco." All I could do was listen as her and Iciss talked. I had introduced them sometime ago.

"Madi can you sit wit him while I go to tha cafeteria?"

"Of course."

"Oh Papi who could want to hurt you? At first when Iciss called to tell me, I thought it was Flacco until she said it happen in Philly."

"Madi it was that snake ass Nigga I need you to kill him."

"I'm going back home I can no longer be around him and since you're now in this coma that I know you will come out of, there's no need for me to stay wit him."

"Yes there is Madi kill that Snake Ass Nigga!"

"I'm sorry Madi did you want something?"

"No I already ate but thanks anyway. Iciss I'm going home, so can you keep me updated on his condition even if nothing changes?"

"Of course I will."

"You be strong Papi and come back to us."

"I will come back Madi I promise you I will."

Madi kissed my forehead, then walked out.

"Baby I'm going to be right here when you wake up."

"Tank what's up?"

"What up Maze?"

"You look like you doing pretty good that means biz-ness is doin' well."

"Thanks to you guys."

"You know we couldn't leave tha game and not make sure you weren't straight."

"If only yall had let me kill Milan years ago we wouldn't have to do it now."

"I know but at tha time, he was loyal."

"I respected that, but I always knew he was a snake in tha grass."

"I haven't been able to find out where Milan rest his head but I do have some people that's close to him addresses."

"A'ight we gon' hit his block first to bring him out."

Tha first block we hit was 8th and Masters we laid tha whole block down no questions asked; of course there were a few casualties along tha way.

"Make sure you tell ya boss that this is just tha beginning unless he shows his face!"

When we were about to leave, I wanted to be sure a message was received so I put a bullet in tha head of tha guy that was doing all tha talkin'. By tha end of tha night, there were a lot of dead bodies and bloodshed.

"Tank if this doesn't get his attention then we'll take it to tha next level."

"We'll be back up tomorrow." On tha way home I got tha call I knew would be coming.

"Hello."

"Do you think you can get away wit this?"

"Now that I have your attention."

"My friend you put yourself in a bad situation."

"You think so?"

"I know so."

"Milan this is nothing compared to what I'm going to do, trust me.

When I'm done you wish you hadn't killed my brother."

"My friend you'll be buried next to him, I promise."

"Never make a promise you can't keep. Now if you want to be a man and show ya face, then we can stop all tha games but if not, you will be sorry!"

"My friend I want you to remember you started this."

"No, you started this," I said hanging up.

"We have to make sure everybody is on point. I don't want nobody to be caught slippin'."

We already started making phone calls to put everybody on tha same page. Over tha next few days it was pretty much tha same thing us wrecking havoc on Milan's blocks. He tried to send some people down, but they were all killed.

CHAPTER 19

Heem in a Coma

"Madi, when do you plan on coming back?"

"I don't know my mom is really sick and I need to be here for her."

"I know you do and I respect that I just miss you, that's all."

"You have my number so you can call."

"I will, but you do tha same."

"OK I have to go," I said seeing Iciss was calling, "hello Iciss."

"Hey Madi"

"Is there any change?"

"No I just wanted to call and let you know that."

"Thank you and keep me posted."

"I will."

"How are you holding up?"

"I'm trying to stay strong for him."

"Make sure you keep talking to him because he can hear you, and your words will bring him back to us."

After hanging up with Madi I held Heem's hand and begin to talk to him again.

"Heem I love you so much, I just want you to come back to me."

It hurt me to see Iciss in so much pain, but no matter how hard I tried, I just could not open my eyes.

"Look at you, you done turned Heem's room into ya office."

"I'm not leaving his side until he wakes up. And I don't want to hear that he's not going to."

"I wasn't going to say that."

"I'm sorry Jade I'm just a little stressed out right now."

"You have every right to be so don't apologize. Mommy told me to check up on you."

"I just talked to her not even 20 minutes ago."

"You know how Mommy is. What are you working on?"

"My closing arguments for this trial on."

"Look at my brother, I hate seeing him in that bed like that."

"Me too. Did Ahmad make his move yet?"

"I think so. He didn't come home to early this morning."

"Wow so Ahmad is back at it."

"Iciss Ahmad had that look in his eyes he had when he was in tha game before, and it really scares me."

"I know he's been out tha game for a few years but you should be used to that."

"Iciss you don't understand he's not going to stop until he's dead or Milan is."

"Well, I hope it's Milan that ends up dead. My heart can't take anymore."

"Don't worry ya pretty little heart. I'm not going nowhere."

We both looked up to see Ahmad and Craig standing in tha doorway. I ran to Ahmad giving him a hug.

"Don't worry Sis he's going to pull through, he's strong."

"Iciss he did tell me to let you know that he loves you." As soon as Craig said that my tears started like a waterfall.

"Heem I need you please come back to me." *It hurt me to hear Iciss crying knowing I couldn't do anything about it.*

"Heem you have to pull through I need you Big Homey. If you don't there's no telling what I'll do it's because of you that I'm grounded, you saw something in me that nobody else did."

"Potential Craig, that's what I saw if it weren't for you, I wouldn't be here fighting to come back I'd already be 6 feet under."

For tha next month, it was pretty much the same thing Milan was still not showing his face so we kept tha coroner busy. I was back in tha game and I had to say I was impressed at how Heem had took over and change things up.

"Ahmad I got Sly trying to track down Milan so if he even walks to tha corner store we'll know."

"Thanks Maze."

"For what?"

"Helping me out wit this. Come on Ahmad we family I'm gon' ride wit you no matter what; you should already know that by now."

"I do and I also wanted to get your opinion on something."

"What?"

"I got a Connect on some heroin we can lock River and 3rd down."

"It's money in it but you know what kind of heat that brings."

"I know that's why I wanted to ask you before I just jumped in."

"I say cop light just enough to take over those two spots."

"That's all it is then."

"I guess Flacco got word about Heem because he's back trying to open shop again."

"Nah we not gon' have that. I'll have somebody put him down."

"Take Craig wit you go holla at him; if he gets out of pocket send him to tha boneyard." After hanging up wit Maze I called my man in Jersey to place an order for tha heron to get tha ball rolling.

"Where we headed?"

"On tha hill to holla at this nigga real quick." I didn't see him out so I shot by Jubilee.

"Maze was good? Long time no see."

"I know, Hey, have you seen Flacco today?"

"You just missed him."

"Damn how long ago?"

"Maybe 15 or 20 minutes ago."

"A'ight thanks," I said passing him a twenty."

"No thank you," he said while tucking tha money in his pocket wit a smile.

"I was about to come in after you."

"Nah I was cool; he wasn't even in there."

"There goes Fresh, Killer and Tiz."

"Where?"

"Just turned on Scott."

As I pulled to tha corner of 3rd & Dupont they were coming down tha street. I hit tha horn for them to pull over which they did in front of tha park.

"Where yall coming from?"

"Around tha corner looking for Flacco."

"You too?"

"Yeah, I got word he's resurfaced."

"So did we."

Coop and Swish walked up as we were talkin'.

"Big Homies what tha deal is?"

"Yall seen Flacco up here?"

"Hell nah, if we had this shit would be tape off."

"I heard that, if you do so happen to see him call one of us first."

"I rather push his shit back to tha white meat."

"Nah, we need to holla at him first."

"Hey if that's how yall want to handle it then, so be it. If he try to bring his people down to set up shot, Imma air them out, no questions asked."

"I doubt if he do that, but if he does, still hit us." We all got in our cars and pulled off wit hopes of catching up to Flacco.

A few days later, Ahmad had put tha heroin out on third and they were going crazy over it. I stopped at Ray's to get a money order only to have a few people run up on me asking if I had that lock down.

"Maze what it do Big Homie?" I turned around to see Craig standing there.

"I can't call it."

"Yo, this lockdown flying off tha shelf I ran through a brick already."

"What time do you come out?"

"I been out since three."

"Damn it's only 10 o'clock."

"I know, Ahmad might need to buy some more of this A.S.A.P they don't want nothing else."

"Did you call him?"

"Yeah, he said he would hit me back. He was handling something at tha store."

"FACE IT YALL I'M PLAYING BASIC BALL. I'M ON THA BLOCK LIKE 8 FEET TALL."

"This him right here. Asalamu Alaikum."

"Wailakum Salam."

"I was calling to let you know I need some more of that."

"Damn you almost done already?"

"Nah, I'm finished."

"Damn!"

"Tha name is self-explanatory "lock down" that's what I'm going to do."

"Imma call Maze and hit you back."

"He's right here you want to holla at him?"

"Yeah put him on."

"Asalamu Alaikum."

"Wailakum Salam."

"Yo I hit him wit 10 bricks."

"I know it took him 7 hours to dump that and they still lookin' for lock down."

"A'ight, well Imma grab heavy to see how fast it go."

"Did you put some in River?"

"Nah I wanted to see how it was going to do up there first."

"I think it's safe to say it did well."

"I see, do you think he'll be able to handle it?"

"Yeah, Heem definitely picked a winner wit him."

"Say no more, we gonna lockdown dope game up there wit this lock down."

"Here, he said he'll be hittin' you in a few hours, so stay close."

"I ain't going nowhere but to my crib."

"A'ight, you got my number hit me if you need anything call me. Matter fact, I'm gonna shoot by tha hospital to holla at Heem. I haven't been by there in a few days."

"Tell him I said Asalamu Alaikum."

Iciss was on her way out when I got there.

"How are you doing?"

"I'm OK, can you stay here wit him while I go home to shower and change clothes?"

"Of course. Asalamu Alaikum I just came to fill you in on what's been going on since I last seen you. Ahmad hit me wit some dope and Heem they went crazy over that shit. I sold 10 bricks in less than 7 hours. All they want is lock down so when he hits me in a few hours I'm officially lock down 3rd. They not going to have a choice but to buy this or they won't make no money. I'm going to let them eat, but only off my plate so no one will get envious."

"Damn, this little nigga 17 and he on point like a mafucka."

"Heem I know you think you drop jewels on me but I heard and remember everything you said to me as if we just had tha conversation. Youngin' if you are not ready to do time or die this game ain't for you!"

"You were 15 when I told you that."

"Ha! Ha! Ha! Remember, you had me kidnapped to see if I would hold water I was so mad I didn't have my burner on me, but I guess it's good

I didn't cause Fresh or Tiz might not be here. I'm mad at myself for only hitting that nigga in tha arm."

"Don't be if it wasn't for you I'd be dead. How long have I been in this coma?"

"FACE IT YALL I'M PLAYING BASIC BALL I'M ON THA BLOCK LIKE AN 8 FOOT TALL."

"That's Ahmad Asalamu Alaikum."

"Wailakum Salam. I'll be ready for you in 45 minutes."

"A'ight, I'm waiting for Iciss to come back."

"You at tha hospital wit Heem?"

"Yeah."

"Tell him I love him and come back to us."

"He heard you I had it on speaker."

"OK if you leave before I call, hit my phone and let me know where you gonna be at."

"I gotcha, Big Homie."

"I see Ahmad has taken a liking to you." 15 minutes later Iciss came back.

"Sorry I took so long, but I stopped to get a bite to eat."

"That's cool I enjoy all tha time I get to talk to him."

"Craig thank you for not leaving him."

"That goes wit out question. I'll be back in a few days."

CHAPTER 20

Flacco Found

POP, POP, POP!

"You got it fucked up if you thought you was going to come around here and sell anything."

He tried to speak, but only blood came out.

"SSHH, don't talk," I said, putting my finger up to my lip.

He tried to speak again, I put my pistol on his forehead. Pop!

"Didn't I say don't talk Dumb Ass Nigga? Tell ya boss that Swish said," putting six more holes in his chest.

"This nigga Flacco is a bitch, he keeps sending his workers around to talk for him."

"It don't matter to me, Imma just keep sending them back and body bags til he mans up."

"Fresh wants us to call them if we see him, man, they better hope I don't put his brain in his Fuckin lap."

"Come on let's shoot to Dominican Café, I'm starving."

"I was just about to call Vinny's to order a sandwich but I can go for some red rice and steak."

"Here twist this up."

"Ain't nothing wrong wit ya hands Nigga."

"Oh, you must be driving?"

"Damn I can't win for losing wit you."

We sat in tha car and blew tha Dutch before we went in.

"Ola (hello) Papi."

"Hey Mami."

"I not seen you in a while."

"I been busy."

"They say you say that Papi."

"Mami it's been a lot going on lately."

"Do you want ya usual?"

"Yes, please extra sauce and a side of fried bananas."

"Same for me too."

"Coop you crazy I would've been hit that."

"She is bad as a mafucka, ain't she?"

"Hey, you are a better man than me, that's for sure."

"She wifey material and I'm not ready to settle down. That's tha only reason I haven't pursued it."

"I glad to hear that Papi me was thinking you no interested." I turned to see Maria standing behind me wit my plate of food.

"When I'm ready, you'll be tha first to know, I promise."

"And Papi I promise to be waiting."

In tha meantime, he wanted to take you to tha movies tonight if you have a babysitter."

"Babysitter?"

"Yeah for ya son."

"No No me not have kids."

"I thought tha little boy that be here was ya son. He looks just like you."

"Coop you funny, that's me nephew not son."

Maria had me really thinking about becoming a one-woman man 23 wit no kids. You didn't find that too often especially from a Hispanic woman.

"So, I'll take that as a yes?"

"If he wanted to take me, he would've asked himself."

Coop looked at me as if to say Nigga, you better ask.

"Mami I would be honored if you would go wit me to tha movies."

"No Papi I would be honored to go wit you."

"A'ight, I'll pick you up at 9 o'clock."

"I'll write down my address and phone number for you."

We finished our meal, paid tha tab then left; since tha police were still on tha scene, we decided to just fall back for tha rest of tha day.

"400,000 Whew I never saw this much money besides on TV."

"Me either we been on tha come up since we been dealing wit Tiz."

"We got 200g's apiece not including our re-up money."

"We did this in 4 months, so just imagine in another eight."

"Shit we gon' be worth seven digits like Jerry McGuire "Show Me the Money."" (BEEP-BEEP)

"There's ya wifey."

"Man go ahead wit that, we just friends."

"Nigga she come pick you up damn near every night and drop you off in tha morning."

"And we just cool."

"Let me ask her, I bet she won't say that."

"Ask her."

"Bet a hundred."

"Nah."

"Yeah I know."

"Nah bet two."

"It's a bet, hey Val, I see you back to pick ya man up."

"Shut up Bones, we just friends."

"I tried to tell him that," I said wit my hand out.

"I got you."

"Don't got me get me."

"Come on you got me holding up traffic."

"Fuck 'em they can wait."

"Yo pull that shit over!"

"Let me pull over."

"Nah stay right there."

"Damn Homey tell her to pull that shit over."

"Here Nigga take ya doe before we catch a case out here."

I took my money then slowly walked to Val's car looking at dude before I got in daring him to say something else.

"Why couldn't you just let me pull over?"

"I was until dude said something."

"Whatever and don't be betting on me."

"Here," I said, giving her half of my winnings."

"What's this for?"

"Helping me win."

"My house or yours?"

"It doesn't matter but let's get something to eat first I'm starving."

"Me too."

"Shoot over to Ahmad's they still open."

"OOH yeah they got this new chicken, shrimp, and steak cheesesteak that's to die for."

It was a little packed when we got there but I was hungry, so I was willing to wait.

"If it isn't tha girl Val."

"Who are you and how do you know my name?"

"Damn you was that drunk you don't remember me? I am Dom, I was hollering at ya girl Des at Doc B party a few weeks ago."

"Oh yeah now I remember you, you look a little different wit out ya cast on."

"I know right."

"Are you going to order?" Frog asked.

"Nice seeing you again I'll let you order; tell Des to get at me," he said walking out.

"What was that all about?"

"What?"

"Frog if you don't know, then neither do I."

"Frog what's up?"

I turned to see who was talking, "What's up Fresh?"

"Same shit."

"Still no progress on Heem?"

"Nah me and Tiz just came from seeing him."

"He's a soldier he'll pull through."

"I know he will. It's just been 5 months and tha doctor says tha longer he's in it tha more likely he won't come out of it."

"Fuck them doctors he'll be back, trust me."

"A'ight be easy. I'm about to get outta here."

As I was saying that Tiz and Fire came walking in.

"I see you wanted to come get some of this good food instead of that bullshit Benny's, Big Scoop."

"Ain't nothing bullshit about Benny's."

"He ain't got shit on Ahmad's."

"Maybe not but it's not bullshit; don't act like you never ate from there."

"Not since Ahmad put this here."

"What up Fire?"

"Hey Frog."

"That's why you was in a hurry to leave."

"Like you should talk. I told you I was waiting on my Baby to come pick me up," Fire said wit a big smile.

"And I told yall I was picking up Frog."

"Bitch, you said ya friend."

"We are friends."

"Whatever."

"We are," Frog said in my defense.

"If that's what yall want to claim but I know better."

"Bye, I'll talk to you tomorrow."

"That's right run from tha truth."

"We can't catch a break."

"That's cause they all want to see us together."

"They will but we taking it slow right now."

"Papi I enjoyed ya company tonight; hopefully we can do it again soon."

"How about dinner Sunday night?"

"Only if you let me cook."

"It's a date then," I said pulling up in front of her house. She gave me a kiss on tha cheek, then got out tha car.

"Papi is there anything special you want me to cook?"

"I'm not a picky person as long as it's good."

Since it was only 10:30, I decided to head to tha block instead of going home; when I pulled up Swish was on tha porch, smoking a Dutch and drinking Remy.

"Nigga, I know you didn't pass up on that ass to come to tha block?"

"I didn't try to hit plus we got a dinner date Sunday."

"Oh I see you trying to wife Maria."

"Maybe I gotta see if she passes tha wifey test."

"How many times I gotta tell you just because a broad gives it up on tha first night doesn't mean she's not wifey material she might just be feeling you."

"And how many times do I need to tell you if she gives it to you she probably gave it to a lot of other Niggaz on the first night too. Don't get me wrong if she fails and tha shot is good I continue to hit her off."

"I heard that Playa Playa."

"Nah, that's you wit all tha broads."

Man, you know Cassy came through while I was talking to Jane."

"Word."

"She tried to snap, but I had to let her know that I was single and could talk to who I wanted to."

"Wow."

"She left talkin' bout don't call her phone, no more than 30 minutes later, she was calling my phone."

"What did she say?"

"I don't know I didn't answer, fuck her."

"Swish you better be careful you know she psycho."

"She can do something dumb if she want they'll be looking for her."

"Nigga, you crazy."

For tha next few hours money was flowing like crazy.

"Oh Shit."

"What's up?"

"Ain't that tha Nigga Flacco right there?"

"Where?"

"In tha car at ths stop sign."

We ran to tha corner to see which way his car was going. He made a left on fourth so I knew he was going to Jubilee. Just to make sure, I ran to tha corner.

"Yo, let's pop his top."

"Nah we need to call Fresh."

"We'll call him Imma make sure he doesn't leave before they get here."

"Aye Fresh ya boy Flacco up here."

"Damn call Maze, I'm not around."

"A'ight."

"Hello."

"Maze this Fresh."

"What's up?"

"I just talk to Fresh but he's not around so I called you."

"Is everything good?"

"Nah that Nigga Flacco up here at tha bar."

"Don't let him leave I'm a few minutes away."

Flacco was on his way out as Maze was pulling up.

"Don't say nothing just walk," I said putting my pistol in his side and walking him to Maze's car.

"Make sure he ain't holding before you put him in tha trunk."

"What's going on?" (Smack)

"Shut up Mafucka!"

"Do you need us to go wit you?"

"Yeah."

On tha way to wherever we were going Maze made a few calls to let everybody know to meet him at tha chill spot. Once we got to tha spot I knew that Flacco's chances of surviving were little to none. We opened tha trunk and he tried to jump out but was met by a .45 to tha head which knocked him out cold. By tha time he came around Fresh, Tiz, Ahmad and some female had joined us.

"Maze did you call Craig?"

"Yeah he was at tha hospital so I told him to come straight here once he left."

"What tha hell is going on?"

"Listen, we told you about trying to set up shop and here you are again."

Madi stepped out of tha shadows.

"Madi, what are you doing wit these people?"

"These people are my people."

"You bitch!"

"Ms. bitch to you Cocksucker!"

"All that I've done for you and this is how you repay me."

"It is what it is. It was just a job for me Papi nothing more."

"You bitch!" She took her pistol out. (Smack)

"Didn't I just tell you Ms. bitch."

"If I make it out alive, I will kill you."

"Well, I guess I won't have to worry about that."

Ahmad started asking him a lot of questions not giving him a chance to answer one before he ask tha next.

"I'm going to ask you one more time who are you working for?"

Before he could say anything Madi shot him in tha kneecap.

"AAAAAH SHITTTT you stupid bitch!"

"Put this over his head," Ahmad said handing Fresh a black pillow case.

Craig came in 10 minutes later.

"Sorry I'm late but I was at tha hospital busting it up wit Heem."

"Did he just say he was at tha hospital wit Heem."

"So who is tha mystery man under there?"

"Flacco."

"So you finally caught up wit him huh?"

"Yeah."

"Let me get a look at him."

Tiz snatched tha pillowcase off. "Mafucka!" Craig yelled while choking Flacco.

It took Fresh, Tiz and Maze to pull him off and when they did, he pulled his gun and put it to Flacco's head.

"Craig don't shoot him!" Ahmad yelled right before he was about to pull tha trigger.

"Nah Ahmad fuck this Nigga."

"Craig you know him?" Tiz asked.

"This is tha other mafucka that hit Heem up wit Milan."

"Are you sure?"

"Positive," he said, wit tears running down his face.

"I promised Heem if I saw you or ya uncle, I would kill you both."

"Uncle?"

"Yeah, this cocksucker is Milan's nephew."

"Well we can't kill him yet," Ahmad said, pulling out his cell phone.

"Ola my good friend."

"Let's cut out tha bull shit Milan I believe I have something that belongs to you."

"I doubt that."

"Are you sure about that?"

"Positive."

"You hear that Flacco your uncle wants you to die."

Upon hearing his nephews name Milan instantly knew this wasn't a joke.

"What do you want?"

"You."

"Me?"

"Yes you for Flacco if not, he dies right here right now."

"How do I know he's not already dead?" He put tha phone up to Milan's nephew ear.

"Uncle."

"Are you a'ight?"

"Yes I."

"That's enough now what are you going to do?"

"Where do you want to meet?" I gave him tha directions, then hung up.

"You know he's gonna have a thousand men wit him."

"I know and we'll have a surprise waiting for them also."

"So we gotta let this piece of shit live?"

"Just for a little while."

"Man, fuck that!" Craig said, taking his pistol and smacking tha shit out of Flacco repeatedly. Once I saw, Flacco was unconscious, I pulled Craig off him.

"Ahmad please let me put a hole in his head."

"You will but not right now."

"Do you think he'll be able to find tha address?"

"He should have GPS if not, he'll be making funeral arrangements."

"They're gonna need to do that anyway."

CHAPTER 21

Heem Wakes Up

"Hey Iciss."

"Hello Ms. White, how are you doing today?"

"Fine and you?"

"I'm OK."

"I see you braiding his hair up."

"Yeah, I wanted to see if it was long enough."

"He got hang time too."

"Ms. White what you know about Hangtime?"

"Chile please, I got three grandsons."

"Ms. White can you pass me tha bag of rubber bands?"

"He better appreciate you when he wakes up you've been by his side day and night for tha past six months."

"Ms. White i'll be here until he wakes.

"I'm lucky to have a woman like Iciss in my life. I need to wake up." I opened my eyes, but everything was a blur.

"Oh My God!"

"What's wrong Ms. White," I asked turning around.

"Oh My God, Oh My God get a doctor."

I didn't need to say that Ms. Write was already out tha room returning wit Dr. Niles.

"Baby I prayed and prayed for this day."

Dr. Niles put his light on Heem's eyes.

"He's responsive but he won't be able to talk for a few hours."

I couldn't stop kissing him.

"Let me call everybody."

Jade was the first person I called then I called Ahmad.

"Hello."

"Hey Sis."

"Ahmad Heem is awake!" I yelled into tha phone.

"Are you sure?"

"Of course I'm sure I'm looking into his eyes."

"Let me speak to him."

"Tha doctor says he's not going to be able to talk for a few hours."

"A'ight, I'm on my way."

"Is everything a'ight Ahmad?"

"Hold up," he said pulling out his phone, "change of plans. I'll call you when I'm ready."

Then he hung up before tha person on tha other end could respond.

"Maze put him in tha back room, strip him naked and lock tha door."

"Ahmad what's up?"

"Heem." Everybody's face asked what their mouths wanted to.

"No he's not dead, he just woke up."

"WHEEEEW I knew my Big Homey would pull through," Craig said jumping up and down, "that's what tha fuck I'm talkin' bout."

"AAAAAAH!"

"What is all the noise about?" Maze asked.

"Heem is awake."

"Hum-Du-Allāh."

"Let's go to tha hospital."

"This calls for a celebration tonight."

"What we gone do about Flacco and Milan?"

"I think Heem would love to be the one to send them to tha boneyard."

"I think you might be right about that Craig."

By tha time we got to tha hospital, everybody was there.

"Asalamu Alaikum."

"Wailakum Salam," Heem said wit a very hoarse and raspy voice.

"You had ya big brother worried, but I knew you would pull through."

"Milan and his nephew Flacco did this to me."

"I know."

"How do you know?"

"Craig told us what happened so I came out of retirement to hunt Milan down."

"You did that for me?"

"Of course."

"Did you find him?"

"No but there's been a lot of bloodshed in Philly not to mention we got Flacco at tha spot."

"Word?" Heem said excited. "Come on you talkin' to me. I know I've been out of tha game for a few years but I'm still Ahmad."

"I heard that."

"When will you be able to leave this place?"

"Tha doctor ran a few tests so once the results are in, I should be able to leave."

"As long as nothing's wrong," Iciss added.

"Well, in that case, you would be free to leave in a day or two," Dr. Nile said walking in wit his clipboard in hand, "your CAT scan showed no damage to your brain which is always a good thing."

"What about my voice?"

"That should be back in a few days."

"I thought you said a couple hours?"

"That was before your test showed you have a sore throat which is common. Well, let me leave you, but before I do, let me say you have a good woman and supportive family."

"He didn't have to tell me I already knew that."

"I love you Quaheem Jones."

"I love you more."

"I doubt that."

"Heem she was here tha whole time."

"I know she turned ya room into her office for tha last six months."

"Damn you really do love a brother huh?"

"Boy you better stop playing wit me before you seriously get hurt."

After about an hour everybody decided to leave so Heem could get some rest.

"I can't wait to get outta here so I can settle tha score wit Flacco and Milan."

"Don't worry they're going to get what's coming to them soon enough."

"I know the first thing Imma do when they release me."

"What's that?"

"Make love to you."

"Good cause I can use a shot of that myself."

"We can go in tha bathroom for a quickie."

"Boy you Crazy."

"No I'm serious."

"Somebody might come in."

"So." I was almost tempted til Ms. White walked in.

"I know he'll be leaving in tha next day or two and I'll be off, so I wanted to give you my number if you needed anything call me."

Me and Ms. White had gotton real close over tha past six months so I knew I would definitely be using her number even if it's just to say hi.

"I see you two have developed a friendship."

"Yeah she was very supportive at times when I didn't think I would make it."

"Tha crazy thing is it was like I was here, but nobody could hear me."

"The other doctors said we should pull tha plug but I wasn't having it. I knew you was coming back to me."

"Yo, I can't believe he came outta that coma."

"Me either, I'm not going to lie I thought he was never coming outta that shit."

"That goes to show he wasn't ready to die."

"So how do we get Milan wit out having to kill all his men."

"Simple Tank called me a few hours ago to let me know he has Milan's daughter."

"In that case it is simple."

"Do you want to make tha call or should I?"

"I'll do it," Ahmad said, taking out his phone.

"Hello."

"I was waiting on your call."

"Yeah now that you have it this is what's going to happen you're going to meet me alone."

"We've already established that."

"Yes and knowing you, you'll have a lot of your men wit you but I'd advise against it if you want to see your daughter alive again."

"My good friend you don't have my daughter."

"Are you sure about that? Make a call then call me back."

10 minutes later, Milan was on tha phone trying to negotiate.

"OK My friend you win."

"This isn't a game."

"How much do you want for tha safe return of my daughter?"

"Ha! Ha! Ha! You think this is about money I don't need ya money. I'm going to let you think about it then call me back."

"Ahmad why not take his money?"

"I don't need that shit."

"Well I'll take it," Tiz said.

"I bet you would."

"Damn right Fire's birthday is coming up and I wanted to get her that new Audi A-8."

Ahmad's phone started going off.

"Yo."

"Listen, I'll give you 2 million dollars."

"Well, in that case, I'll take that 2 mill and you."

"A'ight, give me two hours."

"Cool but you better be alone or she will die understood."

"Yeah, please don't hurt my daughter."

"Come alone and she won't be. You have my word."

"OK."

I gave him tha address Tank had given me. As soon as I hung up, I called Tank to let him know to be expecting him in two hours and that he was to take 500 thousand for his troubles.

"Ahmad I don't need money for doing this."

"I know but I want you to have it."

"You've given me enough. I'll be running Philly once Milan is gone."

"It's all free money courtesy of Milan."

"Since it's his money, I'll gladly take it and I'll call you once I have him secured."

"I'll be waiting."

"In a few hours Milan will be ours."

It has been 4 days since I was released from tha hospital and to tell tha truth except for tha holes in my chest you would never know I was in a coma for tha past six months. I was ready to get back to biz-ness.

"Baby I am on my way to tha office. I'll call you later."

"OK."

"Love you."

"Love you too."

As soon as she was out of tha door, I called Ahmad.

"Asalamu Alaikum."

"Wailakum Salam."

"How are you feeling?"

"Tayib (good). Did yall get hold of Milan yet?"

"Come on wit tha dumb questions Heem."

"My fault I forgot who I was talkin' to."

"Meet me at tha spot when Iciss goes to work."

"She already left so I'm on my way."

20 minutes later, I was pulling up to tha warehouse. I walked in to find everybody sitting around tha table.

"What up yall?"

"Waiting on you so we can get the party started."

"Wait no longer."

Tiz whistled, and a few seconds later Madi came out wit Flacco and Milan. Anger instantly took over me.

"Take those blindfolds off," I demanded, "what's tha matter? Yall look like you seen a ghost?"

"We killed you."

"Real Niggaz don't die that's why ya boys are dead. Please excuse my ignorance hello," Madi said giving her a hug.

"No problem, Papi I told you to let me kill him Si (yes)."

" I know."

"Papi this is tha man that came to tha house that day."

"Bitch Imma kill you."

"Unlikely, you'll die first and even if you weren't gonna die, you could never kill me Mafucka."

"She's very good at what she does. Flacco pussy makes tha average nigga weak and you were no exception. If it wasn't for Heem you would've been dead so in a sense you should thank him for tha extra months you had to live."

"Milan I would have never expected this from you, I thought we were friends."

"I always put family first Ahmad."

"And so do I."

"I told my nephew not to trust you, but he insisted he could."

"There's a five-letter word for that P-U-S-S-Y!" Everybody started laughing except Milan and Flacco.

"Kill us and get it over wit."

"That would be too easy. I want you to suffer like my family did for tha past six months. Madi strip 'em down."

Once they were naked, I grabbed tha surgical knife off tha table and begin to make small slices all over their bodies.

"Put them back into tha room. They should be dead wit in tha next few days."

"Fuck a couple days, POP POP!" Craig said, shooting them both in tha legs, "that should speed up tha process a little.

I got an even better Ideal," Tiz said, dragging Milan in tha back to tha back door.

After throwing Milan inside, he came back for Flacco. You could hear Milan screaming and I could tell by Flacco's face he was scared.

"Just kill me."

"Nah I want you to have an agonizing death."

I personally took Flacco to tha back door. Milan was no longer screaming. When I opened tha door, I couldn't believe it Taz had ripped Milan head from his body.

"I know this nigga didn't just piss on hisself?" Tiz asked walking up.

"Damn when was tha last time somebody fed him?"

"Fresh fed him two weeks ago."

"No I didn't. I thought killer did."

"No wonder he's so hungry. He hasn't ate for over a month."

"Well he'll be full after this," I said pushing Flacco inside.

"Taz was a tiger we had since he was a cub you Niggaz better make sure you feed him at least twice a week."

"Jade wants everyone to come over for dinner Sunday so I would appreciate it if yall would come."

"Is she making that slamming ass Mac and cheese?"

"Yeah probably so."

"Well you can count me in," Fresh said.

"Even if she wasn't Turk gonna make you go anyway."

"Yeah right."

"Don't talk that tough shit in front of us."

"Nothing I won't say in front of her."

"That's what ya mouth says. Madi you'll be joining us won't you?"

"Sure I'm not leaving until Sunday."

"I gotta get back home before Iciss come check on me. She's been doing that a lot since I've been home, not that mind one bit. A'ight I'll holla at yall Sunday."

"Heem let me holla at you before you bounce."

"What up Ahmad?"

"I just want you to know you don't have to rush back."

"Let me find out you like being back in tha game."

"I'm not going to lie it brought back a lot of memories, but my place is with Allāh not tha streets."

"I respect that."

"I'll leave all that in ya hands."

Ahmad tha last few weeks since I've been out of a coma I've been considering gettin' back on my deen as well."

"Hum-Du-Allāh I have more than enough money and a girl that loves me unconditionally."

"That she does, all tha Jones women are like that. Well you better go before you get in trouble."

ALWAYS AND FOREVER EACH MOMENT WITH YOU.

"Too late. This is her now. Hey babe."

"Don't hey babe me where are you?"

"Wit Ahmad."

"Tell my brother you'll see him later and come on home."

"He's a'ight," Ahmad said.

"Tell him I said fall back."

"She said fall back Ahmad."

"Let me see that," he said reaching for my phone, "now what did you say Ms. Jones?"

"Heem told you what I said fall back that's my man and he needs to come home."

"He was on his way home when you called."

"I bet he was."

"Seriously and he would probably be there by now if I wasn't on his phone talking to you."

"Well, smart ass you the one who took the phone if I'm not mistaken."

"Imma kick ya butt when I see you bye."

"Love you too brother."

"I'll see you Sunday."

"A'ight."

"You need to rest."

"I'm well rested. I've been in that coma for six months."

"No need to get mad at me. I'm just following doctors orders."

"I'm not getting mad at you."

I knew she was upset because she didn't say anything else she just left. I decided to go handle something that I needed to take care of anyway. The next few days me and Iciss barely spoke. We were both waiting for tha other to apologize.

"Are you riding wit me to Jade's and Ahmad's?"

"Why wouldn't I?"

"Well I'm leaving in 15 minutes. Iciss how long are you going to play this game?"

"Until you apologize."

"For what?"

"Never mind. I'll be tha bigger person. I'm sorry. Now was that hard?" she asked putting her arms around my neck and kissing me.

"You better stop before we don't make it."

"They won't be mad if we a little late."

"In that case, follow me," I said walking towards tha bedroom. One hour later we were both laid across tha bed exhausted. "Are you gonna get that Ahmad's been blowing ya phone."

"Yeah and Jade has been doing tha same wit you," he said, as my phone started ringing.

"Let's just jump in tha shower and then head over there."

"Sounds like a winner to me."

"He still not answering."

"Neither is Iciss but I'm sure they're OK."

"Yeah you're probably right."

"Come on let's get back downstairs."

"Yall could've waited until tonight for that."

"Turk we wasn't doing nothing."

"My bad, I thought yall were trying to make a little sister or brother for AJ."

"We gave up. I figured it will happen when it happens."

"Yeah, I'm living proof of that," she said rubbing her belly.

"Girl, you look like you due any day now."

"I know and I still have two months to go."

"She looks good pregnant if you ask me."

We didn't," Turks said giving Fresh a mean look.

"Oh boy here we go wit tha mood swings."

"Better you than me I went through it wit Jade."

"Don't start it Ahmad.

A half hour later Iciss and Heem walked in tha door.

"We thought yall weren't coming."

"I fell asleep."

"So did I."

"Yeah right yall was being nasty," Lexis said.

"No we wasn't," Iciss said wit a big smile on her face.

"Auntie!" AJ yelled running towards Iciss wit his arms out followed by Zia.

"Hey nephew, hey Zia, look at you getting all big. How old are you now?"

"Three," she said putting up two fingers.

"Ya daddy gonna have to keep tha boys off you when you get older."

"Please don't get him started," Bre said wit a big smile.

"I'm not going to say nothing. You already know where I stand on that issue."

"I'm glad I don't have no daughter," Ahmad added.

"I wish I could say that Imma kill me of mafucka," Killer said passing Lexis his daughter.

"Daddy."

"What's up AJ?"

"Don't worry I'm a beat 'em up. If they don't act right." We all started laughing.

"Yall laughing, but my grandson is dead serious."

"Jade, do yall have any aspirin? I have a headache?"

"Sit down, Iciss look in tha bathroom cabinet and get that aspirin for

Heem."

"Are you a'ight Ahmad asked wit tha look of concern on his face.

"Yeah, I just get headaches from time to time but tha doctor say it's to be expected."

"Here Baby," Iciss said, handing him tha aspirin and a glass of water. "Thank you."

"You're very welcome."

"Tiz you didn't bring Fire wit you?"

"Nah, her and her girls went to some spa resort wit her job this weekend."

"You don't sound too happy; let me find out you all in love and missing ya boo-boo."

"Fuck you Heem."

"Ha! Ha! Ha!"

"So what if he is, ain't nothing wrong wit it."

"Please don't get her started."

"Shut up Fresh. I'm glad he finally settled down. Come on ladies let's go into tha den so we can talk."

As soon as they were gone, Ahmad started talking.

"Listen since everything is back in order I'm going back into retirement."

"Damn I was kinda hoping you would stay in tha game."

"For what? My work is done."

"Come on my tell me you don't miss tha rush."

"I'd be lying if I said I didn't, but I'm not willing to put my life or Jade and AJ's life in danger."

"I respect that if nobody else does, that's why at tha end of tha year I'm getting out too."

"When did you decide this?"

"When I realize life was too short besides, I have more than enough money to last a lifetime."

"Hum-Du-Allāh."

"Are you sure you feeling OK Heem?"

"I'm cool it's just time; I think about Iciss as well as myself she deserves more than a hustler."

"Wow I never would have thought I'd hear you say that."

"I just don't want to put her through what she just went through the last six months."

"Respect Respect." I watched as a smile crept on Ahmad's face.

"Dinner is ready!" Bre yelled.

"Good cause I'm starving."

"Hey Heem let me holla at you for a sec."

"What's up Ahmad?"

"I just wanted to say I'm proud of you."

"What for?"

"What you just said shows a lot of growth."

"Ahmad I've had enough. I'm ready to start my own biz-ness, settle down, maybe have some kids later down tha line."

"Are yall gonna join tha rest of us or what?"

"Here we come now."

"Is everything a'ight?"

"Yeah couldn't be better."

After we ate, we all sat around talking.

"So Heem I hear you about to exit out tha game."

"Yeah in a few months I'm done."

"I know you got to be loving that Iciss."

"Actually, this is tha first I've heard of it."

"Well, that's because I just decided it."

"I need something to drink would anybody else like something?"

"No."

My phone started ringing now why would he be calling me?

"Hello."

"Hey sexy."

"Why are you calling my phone Dash?"

"I wanted to check tha status of my peoples case."

"Then you need to call him if he wants you to know he'll tell you."

"Damn is like that?"

"Biz-ness nothing personal."

"How bout you let me take you to lunch or dinner one day this week?"

"I don't think so."

"Iciss I remember a time when you used to love me."

"That was before you decided to cheat and we both moved on since then."

"Maybe you have but I haven't. I still have feelings for you."

"That's too bad I'm wit Heem and we're happy."

"Are you really?"

"Look I don't have time for this, so please don't call my phone anymore."

"Whatever you know you still want me."

I didn't even respond and I just hung up. He had tha nerve to call right back.

"What!"

"Is that any way to answer your phone? Especially for a friend."

"I would appreciate if you wouldn't call my phone anymore."

"I want to give you some biz-ness. Call my office set up an appointment. Iciss you know as well as I do that you still love me."

"Please."

"When you get tired of him I'll be waiting and trust me you will get tired."

"You must be making tha Kool-Aid."

"Call my office goodbye."

"You a'ight?"

"Yeah I'm good why?"

"You just seem a little upset."

"That was Dash."

"Who?" I asked, pretending not to know who she was talking about.

"Dash my old boyfriend."

"Oh."

"Don't you want to know what he wanted?"

"No I trust you."

"He's trying to get back."

"Is he?"

"Yeah but he doesn't have a shot."

"Does he know we're still together?"

"Yes."

"So he just disrespected me then?"

"Baby don't worry he don't have a shot."

"That's not tha point, but don't you worry about it I'll talk to him."

"Heem don't." As soon as he looked at me, I knew there was no talking him outta it.

"Is everything a'ight in here?"

"Yeah we cool."

CHAPTER 22

Heem's Spots Hit

"Don't nobody Fuckin' move!"

"Yall heard him hit tha floor and please don't make me say it twice."

"You get up. You're going to put all tha work and tha money in this duffel bag, if you try anything slick, I promise they'll be wearing ya face on a T-shirt."

"Do you know who you're robbing?"

"Nigga do it look like I give a fuck?"

"You might want to rethink this."

Ha, Ha Heem got you soft Niggas shook."

He tried to make a move which I have expected. Pop, Pop.

"Yo, what tha hell is going on in there?"

"This dumb mafucka tried some stupid shit so I shot him. He lucky I didn't push his shit back now filled tha duffel bags up."

Once we had everything, we left tha same way we came thru, tha back.

"Who's spot was that we hit they was holding," John said as he counted the last of tha money.

"Heem"

"Heem Nigga is you crazy?"

"Fuck that Nigga!"

"I know this wasn't about that bitch Iciss."

"Nah," I said lying.

"Whatever it wasn't, now give me my share I got something to handle."

"Aye John, I hope this doesn't come back to bite us in tha ass."

"I know and Fresh is my blood."

"We better sit on tha work for a while til tha heat dies down."

"I'm wit you on that little homey."

"What do you mean Bam got shot and somebody hit tha spot?"

"Did you get a look at them?"

"Nah all of them had on masks."

"How many was it?"

"Three and they knew it was Heem's spot."

"How do you know that?"

"Bam said they said it."

"So somebody has a death warrant. A'ight let me put my ear to tha street see what I can come up wit."

"Cool, if I hear anything I'll make sure to call you."

"So what did he say?"

"Nothing but whoever did it knew it was one of our cribs."

"That could only mean one thing."

"What's that?"

"They don't value life because if they did, they would've never robbed one of our houses."

"We'll be able to find out who it was once they try to sell tha work since we're tha only ones in tha city wit it."

"They'll probably wait until it dies down before they put it on tha streets."

"Hey Chas."

"Hey girl, ya 9 o'clock just called he said he would be a few minutes late."

"OK just call me when he comes in."

"Will do, oh yeah, Jade said to call her if you want to do lunch."

"She must of been reading my mind, I was gonna call her to see if she wanted to do lunch wit us."

"Hello."

"Hey Big Sis."

"Chas gave you my message I see."

"Of course she did but I was gonna call you anyway to see if you wanted to do lunch wit me and Chas."

"Sure, do you want me to meet you at ya office?"

"I can pick you up if you want; it doesn't really matter to me."

"A'ight, what time should I expect you?"

"Between 12 and 12:30."

"A'ight I'll be waiting on you."

"Iciss."

"Yes."

"Your 9:30 is here."

"Send him in."

"Are you sure?"

"Yes, why?"

You'll see."

"Go ahead in Dash."

"Good morning Ms. Jones."

"Dash what do you want?"

"To talk to you."

"Is it concerning a case?"

"No."

"Then we have nothing to talk about."

"You told me to make an appointment."

"Concerning a case not for personal reasons."

"I just want to talk to you Iciss."

"Dash I have a busy schedule. I don't have time to play games."

"Who's playing games? I know I messed up and I'm sorry but I want you back in my life."

"I'm sorry but that is not going to happen. I love Heem and have for a long time."

"Bitch you was in love wit him when we were together!"

"First of all, who you calling a bitch? Secondly, I never let my feelings be known because you were my man and I would've never disrespected or cheated on you no matter how I felt unlike you; now please leave."

"That nigga will never love you like I do or do tha things I did for you."

Chas busted in tha office wit her stun gun in hand.

"Is everything OK Iciss?"

"Yeah, he was just leaving."

"When he breaks your heart don't come running back to me."

"Oh trust me if that happens you'll be tha last person I call."

"You say that now."

"And Dash I hope you don't but if you get cased up please don't call me because I won't represent you."

"Fuck you bitch," he said slamming tha door on his way out.

"What was that all about?"

"He's been trying to get back."

"You need to tell Heem."

"He already knows."

"Dash needs to fall back. He had his chance and he blew it."

"I know, would you believe I told him that I was in love with Heem when we were wit each other."

"Bitch no you didn't."

"Yes I did."

"Ouch, I know that hurt."

"Oh well, he didn't care how I felt when he cheated on me."

"They say you never miss a good thing until it's gone."

"He'll get over it I did."

"Here comes your 10 o'clock appointment."

"Chas thanks for having my back."

"Always you know we do it BFF. Follow me this way please."

"Hello Ms. Jones, my name is Alex Young and I've been charged wit trafficking cocaine 50 to 100 grams."

After he explain to me what happened I had no doubt in my mind that I would beat them in a suppression hearing."

"A'ight, I'll put a motion to suppress in and we'll go from there."

"How much? For your Rule 16 and suppression 3,500. If we have to go to trial another 3 grand."

"Damn!"

"Damn, what?"

"That's cheap for somebody who supposed to be tha next Cochran."

"I was giving you a play for that price."

"Do you think you can get me a sweet plea?"

"Plea?"

"Yeah."

"I'm sorry I think you need another attorney."

"Why?"

"I don't do pleas unless we're in a no-win situation."

"So are you saying that I'm in a win situation?"

"Like I said, if you want a plea, you need another attorney because I am not the one, believe me."

"I'll take my chances wit you," he said pulling out a wad of money.

After he counted out 3,500 he put tha rest back in his pocket then waited as I wrote him out a receipt.

"Thank you Ms. Jones."

"I'll call you when we get a court date."

After I finished wit my 11:30 I was more than ready to eat. "Chas."

"Yeah."

"Are you ready to go to lunch?"

"Yeah give me 5 minutes. I need to finish typing this letter up."

"A'ight, Imma call my mom so she can be ready when we get there."

"I know you ain't go cop a new car?"

"This ain't nothing but a Crown Vic."

"Yeah but it's a 08 Crown Vic. Why would you buy that and draw attention to yaself?"

"Nigga I already had doe before this shit."

"Dash I think you want a bullet in ya head."

"Mafucka I'm not worried about that nigga. He bleeds just like me."

"All I'm saying is be smart about this shit."

"Nigga Imma do me and I advise you two Niggaz to do tha same."

"Oh trust we gon' do us we just gonna be smart about it."

"Mafucka if you that scared get a gun."

"Already got one," John said lifting up his shirt.

"Well man up then Nigga!"

"Fuck you Dash, you sucka for love ass Nigga!"

"Wit out warning Dash smacked John wit his pistol, knocking him out cold.

"When he wake up, tell him, I said don't ever disrespect me again."

After he left, I threw cold water in his face to wake him up.

"You a'ight?"

"What happen?"

"Dash hit you wit his pistol."

"He got tha right one now."

"What you gonna do?"

"I should tell my cuz that it was him who hit their spot."

"That's gonna put us in tha middle."

"Nah I'll just let him know that we didn't know who spot it was until recently."

"A'ight, but then we got to get tha money back."

"Not if we only got drugs and Dash got tha money."

"Fuck that Imma off that Nigga for disrespecting me like I'm sweet like that."

"Chill I got an even better ideal." After he ran it by me, I had to admit it was a hell of a plan.

"Let me call Fresh so I can set up a meeting wit him."

"Hello."

"What tha deal Cuz?"

"Who is this?"

"John."

"Oh shit what up Cuz?"

"I got some information you might be able to use."

"Oh yeah?"

"Yeah, where can I meet you at?"

"Must be serious if you don't want to talk on tha phone."

"You can say that."

"Meet me in tha park in a half."

"Cool."

"So what he say John?"

"I got to meet him in tha park in 30 minutes."

"A'ight Imma go wit you if it's cool."

"That's up to you, but let's shoot by tha spot so we can grab that work up."

"Yo, I think my cuz might have some info or who hit tha crib."

"Why are you say that?"

"He just called and said he had some valuable info for me; I'm bout to meet him in tha park to find out now."

"I'm headed that way too."

"Aye yo Fresh you still wanna play that game for tha money?"

"Nah you got that."

"Nigga Marky D would bust ya ass anyway."

"That's why I'm not gonna play him. I've never been one to just throw money away."

"Yeah cause you definitely would be donating. It would be for a good cause," Marky D said wit a smile.

"Yo there he goes. Let me go holla at him, I'll be back."

"What up Cuz?"

"I can't call it, what's good wit you?"

"Same shit different toilet. So what was so important you needed to meet face-to-face?"

"Didn't one of ya spots get hit last week?"

"Yeah, why?"

"I know who did it."

"Who?"

"Dash."

"Dash are you sure?"

"Yeah."

"Ain't that ya peoples?"

"Not anymore."

"Why are you just now coming to me wit this?"

"I just found out it was ya spot we hit."

"We?"

"Yeah he told me and Chop that he had a sweet hit for us, and you know me, I ain't passing up on no free money."

"So where is tha money?"

"All we got is drugs wasn't no money."

"It was a quarter mill in there."

"I knew that mafucka was lying to us, that explains tha new car."

"So what made you tell me."

"Fresh you my blood our moms is sisters I would never hit one of ya spots knowingly. When I confronted him about it, he stole me and hit me wit his pistol. I want to kill him myself for even thinking he could get away wit some bullshit like that."

"No we'll take care of it."

"I think he only did it because of Iciss."

"I got tha drugs in my car for you."

"Hold up let me hit Heem real quick."

After he hung up wit Heem, he said that we could keep tha work as long as we help them get Dash which I had no problem doing.

"A'ight Cuz just act like everything is cool and I'll hit you when we ready."

"No problem. Chop let's role-play boy."

"What did he say?"

"He called Heem and they said we can keep tha work if we help them wit Dash."

"Are you for real?"

"Damn, right."

"This is tha jumpstart we needed. It's on now. Let me make this call."

"Who are you calling?"

"You'll see."

"Yo."

"What Nigga?"

"Damn don't say it like that. I just called to apologize for disrespecting you."

A'ight just don't let it happen again."

"Sure thing," I said hanging up.

"I know that had to hurt?"

"You damn right it did, but I had to do it."

"How do you want to deal wit Dash?"

"Death!"

"I know that, I mean do you want me to have my people take care of him?"

"Nah I want him to look into my eyes while I'm taking his life."

"No disrespect, but Iciss must have that bomb ass shot for him to be willing to die for it."

"Ha! Ha! Ha! Funny, you say that because I told myself I know what, they mean when they say killer pussy."

"Well let's get tha ball rolling. Have ya Cuz set it up as soon as possible."

"Already done. He's just waiting for tha call."

"So make it."

"Hello."

"It's Fresh make it happen."

"Are we going wit what we talked about or has tha plan changed up?"

"Nah everything is still tha same except make it 8 instead of 10 o'clock."

"No problem," I said hanging up.

"John, we still on for tonight right?"

"Yeah, that was her letting me know that they would be leaving at 8 instead of 10 and tha door will be unlocked already."

"I know you two Niggaz ain't going on a caper and didn't tell me about it?"

"We figured you was straight."

"You can never have enough paper."

"I know that's right."

"Who's spot is it anyway?"

"One of Heem's spots."

"I really want in."

"Why you got such a hard on for Heem?"

"I just don't like him."

"Because of Iciss?"

"I didn't like him before he started dealing wit her that was just a cherry on top of tha Sundae. Who is leaving tha door unlocked?"
"My peoples."

"You sure this ain't no set up?"

"My folks don't get down like that."

"I'm just asking no need to get upset. I need to go check up on something. I'll meet yall back here at 7 o'clock."

"We'll be here."

"Yo, I can't wait to rock that mafucka to sleep."

"Yeah once we do, Imma hit his stash. He's not going to need it where he's going."

"Sure ya right."

"I need to hit Fresh up so he can set it up. Hey Cuz."

"What up John?"

"We'll be there at 8 o'clock."

"Cool I'll put some money in tha back bedroom to make it look official."

"A'ight, cool."

"When we go in, let's get in and get out. Dash, you check tha bedroom upstairs, Chop check down in tha basement, I'll check these rooms."
While Dash was upstairs, Heem, Tiz, Killer, and Fresh came in through tha back door. I put my finger to my mouth, then pointed upstairs. They slid inside tha pantry, so Dash wouldn't see them when he came down tha steps.

"I hope yall had better luck than me, wasn't shit up there but this necklace," he said, holding up tha chain. Me and Chop both looked at each other.

"We didn't find shit either."

"This shit was a waste of time."

"You sure wasn't nothing upstairs?"

"Yeah I'm sure," he answered wit hostility in his voice.

"Who tha fuck you raising ya voice at Nigga?"

Before he could respond Heem, Killer, Tiz, and Fresh came walking out.

"What the fuck is this?"

"Judgment day," Heem said pulling out his .40 Cal., "so you thought you could get away wit robbing me twice?"

"Hooold up Homey I'm here wit them."

"You a bitch!" Chop shouted. "Look let's cut tha bullshit we told them about you hittin' their house."

"You two Niggaz were there too."

"We told them that to had you told us who spot it was we would of never hit it wit you."

"That money you just got from upstairs give it up."

"I don't know what you're talking about."

"Chop look in tha yard next door and bring that money in here."

Chop left then came back within seconds wit a black duffel bag

"Damn you a snake in the grass."

"Man, hold up I can explain."

"Nigga die wit some dignity," John said now pointing his gun on Dash.

"All tha shit I ever done for you and this is how you repay me?"

"Done for me mafucka all you ever done for me is try to play me. Matter fact." (smack) I hit him across tha bridge of his nose wit my pistol, causing blood to go everywhere.

"Heem let me get that pistol."

"Fall back playboy let me handle this one."

"If you gon' to kill me, then get it over wit."

"Nigga you not running nothing you don't get to dictate when you die so just sit back and enjoy The ride."

"You know she'll never love you tha way she loved me."

"Is that what this is all about? Oh shit, this Nigga is a sucker for love

Ass Nigga." Everybody laughed, and at that moment Dash felt froggy and leaped for tha gun. Pit, Pit, Pit, Pit, Pit Click, Click, Click Heem squeezed til tha clip was empty.

"Call the cleanup crew have them handle this. John and Chop get wit Fresh tomorrow he'll have something for yall, if yall want to get down if not, I'll still respect yall."

"Man, we would love to be on tha team you can trust us."

"You've already proven that."

For tha next few weeks I was making sure that everything and one we're straight since I would be leaving tha game real soon.

"Come on we're going to be late."

"Babe we're always late."

"I know so let's surprise everybody by not being."

When we pulled up to Jade's Fresh and Turk were just arriving also.

"Damn we must be late."

"Oh so you got jokes huh?"

"I know, why can't we just be on on time for once."

"Must be a special occasion." I looked at Fresh who just shook his head no.

"No wonder it's warm out for a December day. Look who's on time yall."

"Everybody is a comedian now I see." We ate dinner than sat around talkin'.

"Can I have everyone's attention."

"Uh Oh Jade is about to give us a speech yall."

"Shut up Bre."

"OK OK let's hear it."

"Me and Ahmad are having another baby."

"We are?"

"Yes I just found out yesterday."

"Yeah I am gonna have a little sister or brother," AJ said excited. Everybody started clapping.

"Excuse me," I said standing up, "I have a little surprise of my own."

"Oh no, don't tell me you knocked up too?"

"Ha, Ha very funny but seriously yall know that in two weeks I'll be outta tha game."

"Yeah and?"

"And since I will I'll have a lot of time on my hands, so I figured I should spend it wit my Baby"

"So you really leavin tha game?" Ms. Sady asked.

"Yeah I need to enjoy my life as well as my money." Iciss sat there all smiles.

"I think somebody is happy wit that decision."

"Damn right I am; I been wanted him to be done, especially after that 6 month scare."

"Well, no more worries." I proceeded to get down on one knee while pullin' a box out my pocket.

"OOH My God! Is that what I think it is?"

"Bitch you know what that is," Chas said clappin'.

"Iciss there are no words that will ever be enough to describe how much I love and care about you.'

"AWWE," Turk said with tears in her eyes.

"Iciss Jones will you do me thee honor of being my wife?"

"Yes, Yes, Yes of course I will."

After I put that 5-karat ring on her finger she gave me tha biggest kiss ever. Unfortunately this happy moment was short lived by tha sound of Killers phone going off. We all could tell by his facial expression that it was serious.

"Whats up, you good Killer?"

He looked at all of us then said, "Fellas we have a real problem. Ladies could you excuse us for a few please."

Once tha ladies left we all waited for Killer to speak. After hearing what he had to say it was obvious that Heem would not be retiring and Ahmad as well as Maze would be unretiring too.

PART 3 INTRO

It's Gon Be Wht It's Gon Be

"Are you sure tht's wht he said?"

"As sure as tha love you have for Bre."

"Damn so that means Milan told his brother if something happens to him find Ahmad." Killers phone went off again.

"Well fellas we now have a face to go wit tha name," he said turning tha phone so we could all see.

"Oh Shit," Maze said looking at Ahmad.

"Wht."

"Whts up? Y'all know him?"

"Unfortunately yes."

"Well who tha fuck is this skinny mafucka?"

"Fresh don't let his looks fool you; this is one of the most dangerous assassins to ever walk this Earth."

"Constango," Ahmad and Maze both said in unison.

ABOUT THE AUTHOR

My name is Jerz Toston, and I reside in Wilmington, Delaware. First, thanks to my fans for your continued support. This is my 10th book titled It Still Is Wht It Is tha continuation of It Is Wht It Is My other eight books are titled Bound By DNA, Wht U Don't Kno Can Hurt U, Trust is Ery Thing, Compromised, Street Dreamz: Ery Thing Ain't What It Seems, Da Game Ain't Fair, Betrayal & Deceit, Who Can U Trust?, and It Is Wht It Is are available now on all on-line-bookstores. Also, you can call my publisher directly at 877.782.5550 and have them shipped to ya door.

Writing books is my passion and I'll continue to give you page-turners. Just call me Ya Fav Author.

YA FAV AUTHOR

JAZZY KITTY PUBLICATION
PRESENTS
Compromised
JERZ TOSTON

JAZZY KITTY PUBLICATIONS
PRESENTS
Da Game
Ain't Fair
JERZ TOSTON

WHO CAN U TRUST?
Author Jerz Toston